infinite

BOOK TWO IN THE INDEFINITE DUET

—————— *the salvation series* ——————

NEW YORK TIMES AND *USA TODAY* BESTSELLING AUTHOR

CORINNE MICHAELS

Infinite
Copyright © 2019 Corinne Michaels
All rights reserved.
ISBN—Paperback: 978-1-942834-44-1

Cover Design:
Sarah Hansen, Okay Creations

Editing:
Ashley Williams, AW Editing

Proofreading:
Michele Ficht
Janice Owen

Interior Design:
Stacey Blake, Champagne Book Design

Cover photo © Perrywinkle Photography

infinite

dedication

To Melanie Harlow, thank you for making me write light books with you so I could hop back on my broomstick for these.

chapter one

HERE'S A LOW BEEPING SOUND BEHIND ME. I HEAR VOICES, but they're so hushed that I can't tell who is talking.

"I can't be the one to tell her . . ."

Someone sniffles. "She's going to be devastated."

"Yes, but it should come from someone she loves."

I hear a soft sob. "It's not like it's going to make it better."

"And do we tell her about Quinn?" Catherine asks, and my confusion grows as I try to figure out why Catherine is here? What about Quinn? Where is he? Where the hell am I?

A deep sigh releases, and I imagine it's Gretchen. She's the worrier. "Maybe not right away."

Yes, it's her. Both of them are in New York, but I don't remember . . .

I'm so tired, and it's hard to follow their conversation. Everything is heavy, and there's pain radiating through my body. I search my memory for some kind of recollection as to what brought me here. I was in the cab, and then I made it to the office. I remember the pain.

Oh, God.

The pain.

It was so intense, as though someone was ripping my insides out. Then the events come back in flashes.

Blood.

So much blood. It was . . . everywhere. I remember screaming as I fell to the ground and then . . . nothing.

I was drifting, trying to find the earth but unable to find anything to tether me.

"Let's take it one step at a time and hope we have answers when she wakes up."

Wake up.

I need to do that so I can figure out what's wrong. My limbs are weighted down, heavy and unable to move. Nothing is working, and my heart starts to race as panic grips me. I need to open my eyes. I need to know what the hell is happening and where I am, but I can't make it happen.

Quiet falls on the room as I hear the beeping accelerate, and then someone links their fingers through mine. My body is limp, and there's this fog around me that I can't seem to break through. Maybe this is a dream?

Yes. That could be it. I need to calm down because it isn't real.

I'll wake up now, right? It's a nightmare.

Wake up, wake up, wake up!

"Ashton, Ashton, it's okay," Catherine says from beside me.

Only, nothing is okay, and if I'm right, the dream is a reality. I fight to find my way through the darkness that holds me down. As much as I don't want to see the light, I have to know about the baby.

"Ash, we're right here," Gretchen says. "Just stay calm honey, you need to relax."

Everything inside me feels like it's being torn apart. All I remember is the chaos. People rushing toward me, the blood pooling around me, and the sheer agony as I was enduring a pain like I'd never known.

"Nurse!" My mother's voice breaks through the panic that is overtaking me.

She's here. My mother and my two best friends are all here, which means only one thing . . . I lost the baby.

The fight leaves my body as I willingly allow the fog to take me. To hide me away from the truth waiting for me. As I drift off, I wonder if I can cry while I sleep because my entire life has shattered, and I don't want to wake up.

Dreams are funny things. They can be both wonderful and devastating at the same time. I'm not sure what is true anymore or how many hours or days it's been. I know that, at this point, even if I could open my eyes, I no longer want to.

When I'm sleeping, the world is right. I'm growing larger with the baby in my belly, safe and secure as only a mother could keep them. My hands rub the spot where I notice a kick as I lean back into Quinn's arms.

We plan our life, build furniture for the nursery, and the ring on my left hand sparkles in the sunlight.

I was able to envision it all.

Quinn proposing to me is another of my favorite dreams. His proposal is one that you write songs about. He takes me to Central Park, and the sun is shining down on us, warming our faces even though there is a slight chill in the air. Quinn holds my hand until we reach one of my favorite bridges. The view is perfect as a family of ducks float in the water below. I can see the grass and a scattering of rocks on the far bank, but the true beauty is the bridge itself. It's old and gray but the carvings are what make it amazing. They are subtle, and yet, they aren't. I could stand here forever with his warmth against my back and his arms a cage of safety.

Quinn turns me around, his hands cradling my face as he kisses me softly. Then he drops to his knee and asks me to marry him.

Of course, I cry, saying yes over and over because he is my heart and he gave me the one thing I want most—our child.

His lips press to my belly, loving the baby we created before he slips the diamond onto my finger.

"Ashton," my mother's soft voice breaks through to my dreamscape. "I know you're there and you're scared. You have to open your eyes now, my sweet girl."

I can hear the worry in her voice. I just want to stay here a little longer, though. It's much better pretending that everything is as it should be.

I need to live in the lie. The lie is nice and inviting. It encompasses me like a butterfly's wings, giving me shelter from the outside world. Feeling? Well, that's too much pain for me, and I've had my fill.

Someone's hand grips mine, the rough calluses make me wonder if it's Quinn. "I need my fighter to come back." Daddy's deep timbre rings out.

It isn't Quinn.

He's the voice I've been waiting for. He's who I need.

Where is he? Why isn't Quinn here?

"I'm worried," Mom says. "It's been two days, and the doctor said she should've woken by now."

My dad's hand pushes my hair back, and I imagine the way he must be looking at me. When I was sad or hurt there was this kindness in his eyes. It was as though my pain was his and he was trying to absorb it for me.

"Ashton, my darling girl, open your eyes. We're right here."

I know it's time to face reality, and I need to find out what is happening with Quinn. No longer does my body feel as though it *can't* respond, I just don't want it to.

I've stayed like this, hoping that Quinn would be here or maybe they'd say something to let me know what's causing his absence, but they don't.

"Do you think she can hear us?" Mom asks.

"She can hear, she's in there, and I'm hoping she'll listen to her daddy and fight again."

Mom's voice is shaky. "I would take all the pain away if I could, my baby. We're all here, we just need you to trust that it'll be okay."

I hear footsteps and then a chair scrape against the floor. "Is she awake yet?" Catherine's voice rings through the room.

"No."

"Would you guys give me a minute with her alone?"

Great. I'm not in the mood for anything that Catherine has to say. Let me sleep. That's all I want.

A few minutes pass, and my bed depresses a second before she takes my hand in hers. "I know you can hear me. I've known it for about a day now, but I've let you keep yourself in shut-down mode. Even Dr. Madison said the medication has worn off and you're holding back." Her voice is soft, but I hear the edge of anger there. "I can't begin to imagine whatever it is that you're thinking and feeling. You've always been the tough one out of our trio, but right now, you don't have to be, Ashy. You don't have to stand tall or not cry. You do need to open your eyes, though. I need you to so that we can talk about this. So, open your eyes, biffle."

My breathing becomes slightly erratic. I already heard more than I wanted to.

However, I have a million questions, and I would rather do this with Catherine than my mother. Mom will fall apart, and I don't want to do that to her.

Slowly, I lift my eyelids, but the light is so bright it forces me to slam them back down.

"I'll close the blinds," she says as she jumps.

I hear the scraping of them gliding and then try again.

This time, I'm able to see her brown eyes and the tear that falls down her cheek. "Hi." Catherine's voice is filled with emotion.

My throat is dry, but I croak the words out. "I lost the baby, didn't I?"

Catherine nods as another tear falls. "I'm so sorry."

I feel the moisture leak down my face, and the pain I thought I felt before is nothing because there are no lies here, only the unbearable agony of losing what I loved more than I ever thought was possible.

chapter two

ASHTON

$\mathcal{C}$ATHERINE'S HANDS GRIP MINE, AND WE BOTH CRY. I CRY for the loss of the baby. I cry because it physically hurts, and I cry because somewhere deep inside me I know there's so much more I don't know about yet.

My heart feels as though it's being torn to shreds, and there's nothing that can stop it. I have to endure it all and pray I'm strong enough to withstand it.

I thought losing my first baby was bad, but that was a brush of a feather compared to this. I wanted this baby. I was going to carry the child of a man who I loved and who loved me back. Why does this keep happening to me?

Why couldn't I be strong enough to carry him or her?

Is it something I did?

Is there something wrong with me?

My heart aches with grief as I try to wrap my mind around it, but it doesn't make sense. This wasn't supposed to be the outcome this time. I felt good. I was doing everything right. Quinn handled me with kid gloves to make sure I didn't strain myself.

So why?

Why? Why, God, why? I let the tears fall and there's nothing I can do to stop them.

Maybe there's some cosmic reason that this wasn't the right time, a reason I was never meant to understand, but that doesn't mean it's fair or that I'm okay with it.

"I wanted this baby," I say as she holds me close.

"I know you did."

"We were . . . ready, you know?"

"I'm so sorry, Ash. I know you guys were happy and there was so much going right, you don't deserve to have it all stripped away."

I nod. "We were happy." *Were* being the operative word because we aren't going to be happy now.

Catherine leans back, but her hands move to cup my cheeks. "I know, and I'm sure Quinn . . ."

My eyes shut as a new wave of grief hits me. I won't be the same, I don't think I'll ever be the same, but Quinn will . . . then it hits me that he's not here. He hasn't been here, and I want to see him.

"Where's Quinn?" I say his name while looking around. My voice is so hoarse that it's hard to hear. She grabs the water beside her, and I see the fear in her eyes.

"Here. Take a drink."

I take a sip of the water, waiting for her to tell me what's going on. "Quinn?" I ask again.

Cat licks her lips, and panic starts to bubble up. Oh my God, did he leave me? Did he come and see what a mess I was and walk out?

Does he hate me the way I hate myself?

"Easy, Ash." Catherine tries to calm me. "I want to explain where he is, but I need you to stay calm, okay? The more you upset yourself the more there's a chance you'll make things worse. You lost a lot of blood, okay?"

I try to calm my breathing, but it's like trying to soothe a frantic beast. I'm sick to my stomach again. I can't handle much more bad news.

"I'll try."

She nods, knowing it probably won't get much better than that. It's all I can promise at this point.

"Quinn is missing."

Missing? My pulse spikes, and my breathing turns jagged and sporadic as Catherine carefully moves closer. "Calm, Ashton. *Please.*"

I place the cup down after taking a few sips, the cool water feels good, but I can't stop the shaking.

Catherine releases a heavy sigh, brushes away the tear that descends her cheek, and then takes both my hands in hers again. "On the day that . . . all this happened . . . you couldn't get ahold of him. Do you remember that?"

I nod once, trying to gather whatever strength I have. That day was crazy, but I clearly remember being on the phone with Mark, frantic when I couldn't reach Quinn. "Yes. So, where is he?"

She looks toward the door and then back to me. "We don't know. The videos that they're piecing together are sketchy. Jackson, Mark, Ben, Liam, and the rest of the team are working on it. Charlie and her team are helping, as well as a couple of federal agents they know, another team of security guys, and anyone else they can ask favors from. There is literally not a soul we know who isn't trying to find him. The only information we have is that he was taken, and so far, there hasn't been contact from the people responsible."

A sob threatens to escape, but I choke it back down. "Why? What the hell was he doing that got him kidnapped?"

"If I knew, I would tell you. But, I swear, Ashton, they'll

find him. They aren't telling me much, mostly because they aren't talking to anyone who isn't involved in the search, but I need you to know that he isn't absent from your side by his choice."

I nod, knowing that I can't speak, my throat is closing in as is the world around me. There isn't anything I can say to adequately describe it. I'm not even sure I'm alive because, surely, this is a bad dream. No God would take my baby and my boyfriend in the same day?

There is nothing I could've done in my life to deserve this level of punishment. Sure, I drank, had sex, sinned, and all that, but I'd like to think I'm a good person. I've loved my family and friends, gone to church when my mother made me, I've helped people become parents when all else failed . . . so, why?

Why would a God who is supposed to love me, punish me this much?

"I can't lose him too, Cat," I say as a fresh wave of tears fall.

She shakes her head, determination filling her gaze. "We're going to do everything we can."

"I need him," I tell her.

"Believe me, I know what you're feeling. It's scary and impossible to find a way to keep hope, but Jackson won't stop until he finds him. I know that's of little solace when your world is upside down, but you have to stay strong and have faith that he'll be back with you."

A few years ago, she was in my place, worrying that she'd lose the man she loved. Funny that the tables have turned now.

Then I think about her advice and how if he does return, what he's coming back to. What if he's living for that child? What if all he's thinking of is us and then he'll find that there is no us—just me.

"And then what?"

"What do you mean?"

My heart can't take much more. I need him now more than ever. We've lost our baby. We didn't plan for it, but it was ripped away and I want it back. I want to hold the precious child that I loved—we loved. It won't ever happen.

"How am I going to tell him I lost our baby? How am I going to explain it when we find him? He's going to be so upset that I did this."

She frames my face with her hands. "Ashton, no one blames you."

"I do." I push her hands away, not wanting her comfort when I'm dying inside. Sure, we can try again later, but that does nothing to help with the pain of right now. This doesn't make losing this child any easier. It's too much.

"Why? You didn't do anything wrong. It happened. We don't always know why, but the doctors are certain it wasn't your fault. You aren't to blame for any of this."

My hand moves to my stomach to touch the baby that isn't there, and I wince. I start to move my hand and notice staples. I thought I was sore, but that was nothing compared to the new wave of anxiety that rushes over me. "What? Why is there? Did I have surgery?"

Catherine's eyes fill with so much sorrow that I weep without even knowing why. Or maybe I do.

If there was that much blood, that much pain, there was something more than just a miscarriage.

"Ash." She tries to control her voice, but I hear it.

"Don't."

I don't want to know what happened or why I have an incision. If she tells me what I think it could be . . . I won't . . . I won't be able to . . . I can't.

"Ashton, just let me say this."

"Cat." I need for this all to stop so I can wake up. "Catherine, please. Please don't tell me."

I beg for her to spare me, knowing the words she's about to say aren't good. They won't be. I can see it in her eyes and hear it in her voice. She's going to wreck my world.

"You need to know."

I already know. I already know it was worse. I already know that the lies I told myself of trying again are gone. How much can one heart take before it gives up? "Is it all gone?"

She nods. "It was a placental abruption with severe hemorrhaging that they couldn't stop."

She doesn't have to say anything else. I let out a cry so loud that three people rush into the room. My mother's eyes are filled with tears, Gretchen's hand is covering her mouth, and the nurse is trying hard to hide her emotions.

I don't care that the pain in my abdomen is so intense or that I probably tore something. It pales in comparison to my heart.

Severe hemorrhaging means they couldn't stop it. No one has to tell me that I'm hollow.

Empty.

Barren.

They took everything, even without Catherine or anyone telling me, I feel it. I will never be a mother.

The life I have always wanted was taken when they removed it from my body. With that much blood and a scar it means one thing: I had to have a hysterectomy.

"No!" I cry out as my mother and Catherine try to keep me calm. "No, no, it couldn't be! No." I thrash as they both talk in soft tones.

"I'm so sorry, baby," Mom says through her tears.

"No, I can't . . ."

"Shh," Catherine says against my ear. "It'll be all right."

No it won't. "I'll never have a baby." My voice is nothing but grief. My child was ripped from me. The man I love is missing. The tattered hope that I held on to a few moments ago was that maybe, in time, I could try again, but even that's gone.

The fight is waning from me as I sob, every emotion possible consumes me as my life alters in one instant. And I realize, I've lost something far greater than a baby . . . I've lost hope.

Six more hours pass.

I don't think or feel anything. I'm numb. Something has broken inside me that will never be fixed.

I want everyone to leave me alone.

My mother hasn't left my bedside, she prays to a God that I don't believe in anymore.

She begs for him to watch over me, but what good is his attention now? No one was watching over anything when I needed them to. Everything was stolen from me, and it'll never be returned.

Catherine came in a little while ago to tell me there's no news of Quinn. Yet another thing that I can't fully handle.

I got him back, only to lose him again. It's as though there's some sick game being played and I've been cast in the role of the loser who believed she had finally won. I had it all. Even things I didn't think I wanted, I got.

I should've known better than to believe it was all going to stay.

"You have to eat, my darling." Mom pushes the tray of food toward me.

"Not hungry."

"Right." She sighs. "And I take it you just want to sleep?"

"Yup."

In my sleep, there's hope. In life, there is none. I have no idea where Quinn is, if he's alive, fed, or in pain. All I know is that, until I do know, I don't really care about anything else.

I want to see his face and have his arms hold me as we mourn the loss of our child. Until that happens, fuck everything else.

Gretchen gets up and comes around the side of my bed. "Do you want me to call Ben for an update?"

Finally, someone who is offering something I give a shit about. "Yes."

"Okay." She grabs her phone and calls him. My eyes are wide as fear and worry fill my body. It's the first thing I've felt in hours.

Gretchen, bless her heart, puts the phone on speaker.

"Hey." Ben's deep voice fills the room.

"Ashton is awake and any update you have on Quinn would be appreciated."

He sighs, but it isn't an unkind sound. "We're doing everything possible. There was a lead a few hours ago that turned out to be nothing. One of Liam's friends with a task force here saw something else, so we're chasing that one now. It's a lot of puzzle pieces we're fitting together. I'm sorry I don't have much more than that. We will find him. It's just a matter of when."

I sniff as I try to hold back my tears. "Thanks, Ben."

"Ash." He pauses and then begins again, "Quinn is our friend and he's family. No one is going to allow someone to take our brother without a fight, okay?"

Gretchen places her hand on mine. "Thanks, babe, please let us know if you have any news. I know that Quinn is your brother, but he's her life, and she needs information."

"I know. I'll do my best."

"We know. We'll talk soon."

I nod, and Gretchen disconnects the call.

Then I close my eyes and wait for the next round of devastating news.

chapter three

ASHTON

W HEN PEOPLE SAY THAT TIME MOVES FAST, I USED TO think the same. Now, I believe quite the opposite. Time is a slow and torturous thing. It has nothing to do but tick slowly by.

I watch the clock on the wall.

Tick.

Tick.

Tick.

On and on it goes, the same sound, the same movement, and yet, as each one passes, something inside me changes.

I'm building a wall. A fortress so tall and so strong that nothing will ever breach it. In there, I'll be safe from any more bad news. However, it isn't going as fast as I want. I need to move the bricks in quicker, make the foundation strong so that not a single pebble topples.

"Ashton?" Clara says softly as she enters. "I came by to check on you."

My mother gets up. "I'll leave you two to talk."

Clara walks deeper into the room, and when I see her pity, I turn my head. I don't want to see any of it. "Ashton, I—"

"Was it you?" I ask softly.

She stops, and I turn to look at her closely. My heart is pounding as I wait to hear if it was my friend who emptied me.

"Yes, and I wish to God it wasn't."

I bite my lower lip, trying to rein in my emotions. "Me too."

I feel a mix of things as I look at my friend. She promised to watch over me and take care of things. I never expected this to be the way it turned out.

"I need to explain," she says quickly. "There was so much blood, Ashton. If there was anything I could do, I would've done it. I swear it. I tried so hard to control it so I could save everything, but . . ."

"You couldn't," I finish for her. Looking at her now, I can see how much this is weighing on her. Her dark brown eyes are dull, and her normally perfect hair is pulled into a low ponytail. She knew, more than anyone, how badly I wanted a child. Motherhood wasn't just a wish for me—it was *everything*.

Losing the baby has been incredibly difficult to process, but losing the ability to ever have a child is impossible.

It's a loss unlike anything I've ever known. She takes a step forward, and in my heart, I take one as well, only I go back. There are emotions I can't process, and this is one of them. I move into my fortress, prepared to shield myself behind what I've been able to build so far.

"I tried."

My hand lifts, and she stops. "I understand, Clara. I don't think you took any of it lightly, and I believe that you did what you could to save what matters to me, and in the end, you saved my life."

The look of relief starts to fill her gaze. "There are options."

I shake my head. "No, not now there aren't."

There isn't a chance in hell I can start to think of options or possibilities. The reality is that I, Ashton Caputo, will never carry a child. I'll never feel the kick of a baby. I'll never know what childbirth is like. I won't ever feel a contraction or work hard to bring that child into the world and be rewarded with her or him in my arms. I need to mourn that loss.

"No, I guess right now there aren't," Clara says with defeat. "You're not alone, Ashton. You have an amazing support team around you."

My team is down a man, the most important one.

"Did you know Quinn is missing?"

"Yes, and I wish there were something I could do to comfort you."

I stop her there. "Please don't. I can't handle it, and there isn't anything that anyone can do or say to make any of this better. The only thing I can focus on is getting out of this place and finding him."

She nods. "I understand that, but you have at *least* three more days in here."

I don't want to be here another second. "I'd rather go home and try to help the guys."

"You won't be any help to anyone if you get an infection or open your incision, and I'm not willing to face Quinn's wrath if I allow you to put yourself in any danger. I need to make sure you're *okay*."

Okay. That's a word that most certainly doesn't describe me. In fact, I'm the opposite end of that spectrum. I'm . . . done.

"Please, don't make me stay here."

Clara's lips form a thin line and a tear falls on her dark brown skin. "You're more than my patient, Ash. You're my friend. If I let you go, it will be the wrong decision. It's only been two nights. With a planned surgery, it's at least five days, and there's no way I'm budging on this."

"So, you want me to sit here for three days, thinking about the fact that Quinn is missing and I'm now . . . this?" The tears fall as a part of my fortress crumbles.

"I don't take any pleasure in this. You need to rest and heal. Your body has been through so much and, while the transfusions have helped, you're still depleted."

"This is . . ."

She moves closer, her hand touching my arm. "Impossible for you? This is incredibly difficult, but if you don't take care of yourself, you're going to end up in a worse condition. Quinn might need you—physically—and if you're recovering and can't help, then what?"

I close my eyes and release a breath through my nose. "Three days."

"*Hopefully* three days, and you have to follow my instructions."

"And if they find him before then?"

Clara gives me a soft smile. "Then we'll figure something out."

She was true to her word. I stayed in that hospital for exactly three days, and now I'm at my apartment, which has turned into some sort of headquarters.

There is equipment on almost every surface, screens are set up in my living room, and people are everywhere.

My mother begged me to come to Jersey, but I refused. I need to be here. I don't want to go to her house, eat her food, and cry. In fact, since that day with Clara, I haven't shed a tear. My walls are high, holding as much in as they are holding out.

"Ash, do you want to lie down?" Catherine asks as she brings in a cup of tea.

"No."

"Okay, do you want to talk?"

"No."

"Are you hungry?"

I turn and glare at her. Catherine has always been my best friend. While Gretchen is, of course, one as well, Cat is who I'm the closest with. Right now, I'd like her to go the hell away. She gave me one day of her not pushing me to talk. I was grateful and thought that maybe it could stay that way. I should've known better.

Catherine wants me to breakdown.

She insists that I need to get it out.

I threatened to break her nose if she didn't shut up.

That lasted a whole four hours.

She sighs, shooting me that look she gives when there's more. "Look, I know you think you're strong and you don't have emotions, but I know you better."

"Good for you. Then you should know that I don't want to express any of those feelings. I've buried them and that's that."

She places the cup on my nightstand. "You know I can wear you down."

"You should go home, Cat. To your baby."

A baby I'll never have.

She shakes her head. Erin is with Jackson's mother. She flew here as soon as she heard what happened. Nina Cole is an angel. I truly don't think Catherine could've gotten a better mother-in-law. That said, I'd rather she go be with her daughter and let me focus on Quinn.

No one has anything new to explain.

All we know is that he's gone. Vanished.

There is some footage of him outside a parking garage, but the person who took him was smart and knew how to avoid cameras, which has left Jackson a bear to be around.

He's concerned, which means Catherine is concerned, and neither of them are making things any freaking better.

"Erin is fine. She's doing great with her grandma, it's you I'm worried about."

"Well," I huff over the word, "you shouldn't be. I'm just fine too."

"You're fine?"

"Yup." I lie.

Cat sits beside me on the bed. "Good. I'm glad you are." Her voice is filled with relief. "Here I was, worried because you lost the baby and Quinn and then you had to have major surgery . . . but you're fine, so I can go back to not worrying."

I roll my eyes at her theatrics. "You can go home too."

"But you're fine. Why would I leave? We should probably talk about the weather or something else that is completely worthless . . . since you're so fine."

My breathing is heavy as my frustration rises. "I'd like to sleep now."

"Sleep is for the not fine. Sleep is for those who want to avoid the major life changes that are plaguing them, which is definitely not you."

She's seriously pissing me off. "Catherine," I say through gritted teeth. "Stop. I know what you're doing, and I don't want any part of it."

"What am I doing?"

"You're trying to get me pissed off enough to talk. I don't want to talk. I want to find Quinn, okay? I want to know where my boyfriend is, if he's hurt, if he's alive, and that's it."

"And what about you?"

It's a loaded question that is completely worthless. I'm safe and cared for, aside from being badgered by the well-meaning friends in my life. I have the use of all my faculties and there's no big mystery as to what is going on in my life. I'm alive, even if I no longer have a heart.

"Right now, I don't matter."

Catherine shakes her head. "You matter to me."

"And I appreciate that, but here are the facts. I lost my baby. I lost any chances of having a baby. I'm . . . I'm broken and the only thing that is keeping me together is being able to focus on finding Quinn. I can't fucking think about what has happened to me, okay? I can't! I can't think about it, Catherine, because if I do . . ." I push down any tears that threaten to come. If they start, they will never stop.

I have to channel this anger and energy somewhere that isn't on the fact that I had a hysterectomy. I can't do it.

I need to worry about only Quinn.

That's all.

"Okay. I won't push you."

"Thank you. Can you please let me sleep?"

She grabs the medicine off the nightstand and hands me the tea. "Here, take these, it'll help with the pain."

I want to throw them at her, tell her there's nothing to help with the pain. There's only anguish and heartache. If there were a pill that would turn back time to before all this happened, I would eat a handful.

"Sure," I say. Arguing with her would be too much effort and I'd rather slip away to deal with the nightmares.

After I swallow it, she tucks me in and then curls up next to me.

It's like we're little girls on a sleepover instead of her trying to protect and watch over me. So many times throughout our lives, I was the one lying with her, trying to soothe her agony. My childhood was filled with joy and love. My parents were my safe haven whereas Catherine's father broke her heart more times than she could count. I wonder if that's why her adult life has been fantastic and mine hasn't been. Am I being punished? Is this some sort of quota for happiness I filled and God is trying to cash in my chips?

We face each other, and I see the tears well in her eyes.

"Please don't start crying," I beg her.

"I was so scared. I seriously didn't know if you were going to make it through the surgery. I don't know if you understand how bad it could've been."

I close my eyes, shoving down the emotions that are trying to claw their way up. "It couldn't be much worse than this, Cat."

Her fingers touch my cheek, pushing my hair back. "I know you feel that way, and I would too, but you could've died, Ashy."

A part of me did.

"I'm still alive, but we don't know about Quinn."

"Jackson will find him."

I wish I had blind faith like that. My eyes drift closed again, and everything becomes a little heavy.

I'm tired.

I want answers, and I want his arms around me, holding me together. We've lost something so precious that we'll never get the chance to have again, and I can't bear the weight of it alone. Quinn and I will never have a child. While he may not have wanted children, there was no denying his excitement about this baby.

Then I remember he bought a ring. He was going to propose to me. We were going to be a family. Everything was perfect and now it's all ruined.

As I slip into the dark, I note the tear that runs down my face. I guess my walls weren't as high as I thought.

chapter four

ASHTON

"**I**'M LOSING MY FUCKING MIND!" I SCREAM AT MARK AND Jackson. "You said you'd find him! You two made him go out there and spy on *your* family!" My finger jabs into Jackson's chest. "It has been *six days,* and we are no closer to finding him! How much more do you think I can take? How much longer before I lose it?"

It's taking every ounce of energy I have to be standing in front of him, but I'm done lying in bed and waiting. It's been almost a week, and we're no closer than the day I woke up to this nightmare.

I'm running on pure rage.

I've had enough.

I want Quinn back. Now.

"I know you're frustrated—believe me, I am too."

"I don't care if you're frustrated. I need him! I need him to come home, and I need him alive. Every day is . . ." I start to sink because I'm so weak.

Having Quinn be missing for six days has felt like an eternity. Plus, I'm still recovering. I lost a lot of blood, and while the transfusion and few days of rest have helped, I'm nowhere close to being healed. The more stress I put on myself, the longer it will take for my body to heal.

Rage may have been driving me, but it can't hold me up.

Catherine's arms wrap around me, and she pulls me to the couch. "I know you're upset, but no one is giving up. You need to rest, Ashton."

I shake my head. "I'll rest when you find him." My gaze moves to Mark and Jackson. "Find him now. He didn't just disappear. He's not a ghost or anything like that."

Shame fills Jackson's eyes. "We're working another lead."

"A lead? And you didn't tell me?"

Mark walks over and squats in front of me. "Listen, Red, we're not telling you anything until there's something to tell. I'm not going to make you crazy by informing you of every tip because it's not going to help you when we follow it and it's a dead end."

"Aren't you guys supposed to protect one another? Isn't that the whole point of this company? You're all former SEALs, and yet . . . what? How the hell is this okay? How are you guys trained to fucking fail?" I know I'm being a bitch, but it's my life that's being thrown around thanks to this.

"Ash," Catherine says with a bit of disappointment.

I don't care. She can be upset that I'm attacking her husband, but at least he's standing in front of her. I'm dealing with all of this alone. "Do you know that the last thing I said to him was that there was something wrong with the baby? Can you imagine . . . if it was one of your wives . . . what knowing that would do to you? How would you feel knowing that you couldn't get to her? Knowing there was something wrong but you were incapable of helping?"

Jackson moves to be next to Mark, and his gaze is no longer sad—it's determined. "I would fight harder than ever, and that's what we're sure he's doing. You might think that the time slipping away is a bad thing, but patience is something we practice. He's not going to strike until it's the right time."

Mark nods. "He's smart and has been trained to deal with situations like this. The reason we don't fail is because we trust each other. There's nothing to be gained by being hasty. If Quinn were dead, we'd know by now."

What they say makes sense, and if I were a rational person, I might care. I'm not, though. My emotions are already stretched thin, and if they stretch any more, they'll snap.

"None of it matters. You were supposed to watch over him. You were supposed to protect him."

"They're doing what they can," Catherine tries again.

I glare at her. "You can say that while you're sitting in the same room as your husband. You can act as though I'm being insane or whatever when the man you love is right here. I can't, Cat. Okay? I can't because he was working for your husband. He was following around your husband's former in-laws, and now the man I love is gone. So, sure, I'm angry and crazy and irrational. Too fucking bad!"

Her eyes fill with tears. In all of our years of friendship, I don't think I've ever snapped at her like that. Jackson moves toward her, but she puts her hand up. "I love you, and I know you're in pain, but no one here is against you. We all want the same thing—him home and safe."

I can't take another minute of this. I'm sitting here, waiting for a smoke signal that isn't in the sky.

Mark takes my hand in his. "You want to yell, Red? Yell at me. I'm the one who told him to do it. I made the decision, and if you think I'm not just as pissed off, you're wrong. I'm raging just like you are, so go ahead and yell."

I open my mouth to do just that because maybe I need to

get it out. Anger I can handle. I welcome it as it pulses through my body. However, when I look at Mark, I can't say anything. The words die on my lips as my eyes close.

I've never felt so out of control.

A heavy breath releases through my nose. "I'm going insane."

"That's what they want." Jackson's voice is tight. "They want division within the team so that we make a mistake, which is why we're doing everything we can to avoid that. The person behind all of this is playing a game."

"Then play a better one and win already," I say and then struggle to my feet, pissed that I couldn't make a dramatic exit.

I awaken from my nap, even more tired than before. I hate myself for snapping at Cat. I hate even more that she came and stayed beside me when she thought I was asleep. I was too upset to acknowledge her and pretended until I actually passed out.

It was cowardly, but each time I start to delude myself into thinking I'm okay, another thing crushes me.

No one came back in after she left, so I'm assuming there are no updates. All we have are leads that go nowhere.

Still, I'd like to hear it from someone.

When I roll over, I see the pile of clothes on the floor, and my heart breaks. I stare at Quinn's shirt, untouched from the day when everything changed.

I know that in the right pants pocket is a ring box. If I were to open it, I'd find a beautiful, sparkly, diamond that I was excited about finding. Only a few days ago, my world seemed to glimmer with the possibilities that were to come.

Instead of life handing me beauty and hope, it gave me the middle finger and laughed as I fell toward hell.

Carefully, I get out of bed and make my way to the pile. I slink down to the floor, taking the shirt in my hands. I bring it to my nose, inhaling slowly and deeply. My eyes close as the cologne that clings to the fabric fills my nose. If only I could wrap my arms around him so I could touch his skin. The way the warmth of his body allows me to feel alive. I would trail my nose down the column of his throat where his musky scent is strongest. My heart swells in hope that I can have that again.

I would hold him so tight, beg for his forgiveness, promise him that I'll do anything if he doesn't leave me after I tell him all we've lost.

He's all that matters to me.

"Come back to me, Quinn," I say with tears falling so hard that I'm sure there will be a puddle around me. I lay down, co-cooning myself around his things. "Please come back. Please fight and live. Please don't leave me. I lost the one thing that was binding us, and I need you to stay with me." My chest aches as I rasp the words into his shirt. "Please don't stop loving me. Just don't be dead . . . and we'll . . . we'll find a way."

While everyone else thinks he's simply missing, I can sense the loss of him completely. The fear that we will never find him is so real that it's hard to breathe. I don't know how much longer I can hold it in. They think that if he were gone, they would know it, but how could they be so sure?

I lie on the cool floor, surrounded by all I have of Quinn, and cry, wishing that my world wasn't falling apart.

"Ashton?" Gretchen's voice is soft as her arms wrap around me as we huddle on the floor. "I've got you," she vows.

I want him home. I want him to comfort me, but he's not, so I have to be stronger than this. Crying won't bring him back. "I'm fine," I say as I push to sit myself up.

She shakes her head. "You are not fine. Stop saying it."

"Don't you start too."

"Start what? Making you talk? Making you say anything other than you're fine or yelling at the people who love you?"

I release a shaky breath. "What would you do?"

"I would talk to my best friends."

She says that, but it's not that simple. "What the hell is talking going to do? I don't want to talk about any of it when nothing will change."

"No, nothing will change, but you can let some of the pain go." Her eyes fill with love and hope.

I could open my heart, tear down the walls, but then I'll be nothing but a vulnerable mess. They'll all go back to their lives and husbands and babies, and I'll be alone here. It's better if I shut it all down and find a way to draw air into my lungs without choking on it.

"The pain I let go will just fill back up and brim over the edge. I don't have a release for it, Gretch. This is nothing like anyone can imagine."

"No, we can't imagine, but we can love you through it."

"You're not who I worry about loving me."

She jerks back slightly. "You're worried about Quinn?"

I'm worried about everything. I reach into the pocket of his pants and pull out the black box. "He was going to ask me to marry him."

She takes it. "He loves you."

I scoff. "He's gone. He's not here, and if he does return . . . he'll find that everything he believed he had is gone." Just like the girl I used to be.

"You need to stop getting ahead of yourself."

No one else will understand this. I was giving him a life he thought he didn't want and then craved more than anything. He was going to have a child, a woman who loved him, and a family.

Explaining this to her isn't going to get her to see things the way they are. Once again, I find a way to bury the emotions I am feeling. I put the mask of understanding and hope back in place. If I can placate her, then this conversation might stop.

"Maybe you're right," I say with a sigh.

She smiles softly. "I don't believe you think that, but I hope you'll hear this. When Quinn returns, he's not going to look at you as though there's something wrong with you. He's going to want to murder the person who took him from you when you needed him most. The blame won't be on you, my friend."

I nod and hope the numbness comes back.

Before I allow it to wash over me, there's a knock on the door. "Ashton?" Mark calls.

"In here." When he opens the door, his eyes are wide and the energy around him is palpable. Gretchen gets to her feet and then they both help me up. "What is it?"

"The lead is viable. We were able to pull a surveillance camera from a few blocks away, and thanks to some friends, we think we've pinned his location."

"How? I don't understand."

He touches my shoulder. "We're going to go in about fifteen minutes. The guys are already gearing up, and we're waiting for one last image so we know what we're dealing with."

"I want to go."

"Go?" Gretchen shrieks. "Go where?"

"I want to go with them!" I say and then turn back to Mark. "Please, I won't get out of the car, but I have to be there. If you find him . . . I can't . . . I have to see him."

Their eyes meet and something passes between them. "Red, I'd love to say yes, but it's not . . ."

"No! She can't go. Jesus, Ashton, you had major surgery!

The only reason you're not still in the hospital is because you bullied your way out of there."

I pin her with a stare so mean I would incinerate her if looks could kill. "I'm going, Gretchen. You can say whatever you want, but this isn't your call." I turn back to Mark. "So help me God, Dixon, if you don't take me to that site where the man I love could be, I'll kill you myself."

He sighs deeply. "Let's see if Jackson got what we need, and you can try to convince him."

In the living room, we find Jackson, Ben, Liam, and two guys I've never seen before moving around and barking orders at each other. As soon as they see me, they stop. Jackson heads toward me.

"Did Mark tell you?"

"He did."

"And she wants to go with us," Mark tosses in before I can say anything. "I already explained that it wasn't my call."

"So it's mine?"

"No, it's mine." I cross my arms. "I would like to know what information you have first."

Jackson sighs. "I'm waiting on a text . . ." he trails off when his phone dings. I see the flash of surprise in his eyes before he recovers. Then he extends the phone to Mark.

"This can't be." Mark sounds almost afraid.

"I don't understand how."

How? How what? It's a text. "What does it say?" I watch the two of them try to make sense of whatever is on his phone. "Hello!" I say as impatience wears me down.

They share a look, and Mark heads to the other side of the room, phone to his ear.

"The photo we just got." Jackson hesitates. "It's . . . we know the person who has him. If this image hasn't been doctored, which I don't believe it has been, then we have to adjust our plan."

None of this makes sense. Whoever took Quinn has rattled them both. "Adjust it why?"

Gretchen's hands wrap around my shoulders. "Jackson, please tell her why this changes anything before she passes out."

Jackson's jaw clenches as his hands clench into a tight fist. "Because it's Aaron."

chapter five

QUINN

"WANT TO TELL ME WHAT WE'RE DOING HERE?" I ASK Aaron. Aaron, the guy who has me tied up after another lovely round of drugs.

Maybe he didn't actually take me. Maybe this is him saving me from the idiot who did because Aaron being the one who abducted me . . . doesn't make a goddamn lick of sense. In fact, I'm wondering if this is all some hazing game that Jackson and Mark have created.

It would be more plausible than this.

"No, I don't think it matters what we're doing, just that we're doing it."

"Okay." I keep my voice even. "Where are we then?"

He shakes his head. "Do you ever wonder how it is that we get ourselves in these messes?" Aaron's eyes dart to the left. "We get out of the navy, go to work for our friends, and end up more fucked up than when we were active duty. It's really interesting how that works out for us. I have all these things that . . . they're crazy, right?"

The only thing crazy right now is him. He's talking to me, but he's looking all around as though focusing isn't working.

"Aaron? Why am I here?" I try again.

"I wanted to save you. Someone has to do it."

"Save me from what?"

He shakes his head. "Don't distract me!"

I look at him, needing to keep him talking despite the throbbing in my head. "Why did you want to save me?"

Then, when his eyes focus on me, there is rage burning in them and his teeth are clenched. "So you don't have the same fate as everyone else."

I have no idea what that means. Who the hell am I ending up like?

As much as I'd like to decode his riddle, my brain is misfiring, my throat is dry, and I'm trying to piece any of this together. I don't remember too much—just small clips of time where there was the misfire with the gun, talk about ransom, death, and escape before I would black out again.

We were both trained by the same people, so he knows all the tricks and protocols. The only thing I can do is ask questions and hope he answers or trips up.

"How many days has it been?" I ask Aaron as he paces.

"Don't worry about it."

I know it's been at least four, and I am able to deduce that I've been drugged for at least three of them.

They don't want a ransom.

They apparently want to keep me here.

"Okay, again, you need to explain why you took me and drugged me."

He shakes his head like I'm a fucking idiot. "To protect you!"

"That's what you said, but from what?"

He turns, his eyes are back to being unfocused.

"Do you know what that place does to people?" he asks.

"What place?"

"Cole Securities!" Aaron bellows. "They take everything from you. Piece by piece, little things will become theirs. First, it might be a limb, they took that from me. But then, your life will dismantle in front of you. My wife, my child, my best friend, who is also to blame in this. They take and never wonder what it will do to someone. Well, here it is. This is what you'll become." His hand sweeps down his body. "Is this what you want? No. No one does. So, I'm helping you before it happens and your *best friend* fucks your entire world."

He means Liam. "So, you thought it best to take me away?"

"How long until someone there decides Ashton should be theirs? Don't you see, Quinn? We're better off away from them. We need to stick together. Your best fucking friend stole my wife."

I would love nothing more than to set him straight and remind him exactly who lost his wife, but I don't. He's talking, he's agitated, and he's armed.

"You think Liam would go after Ashton?"

He shakes his head quickly. "No, he already has Natalie. But the other ones, they're all the same. They find someone who is a little broken, like you and me," his words start to come quicker, almost frantic, "then they make you think they're giving you something, but it's a show. We were all in that ambush, and now I'm the one who has nothing!" Aaron's hands grip the side of his head. Does he really think that the guys left him behind on purpose?

"I get it," I say calmly. "You want your life back."

His eyes meet mine. "I have nothing to get back. I'm half a man who can't stop the sounds. I can't get them to stop, and I have nothing to try for. But you? You have a baby and a woman. We're the same! I had a wife and a baby on the way, but then I went to work for Jackson, and look where it got me. Nothing."

"You have Aarabelle," I remind him. There is nothing I wouldn't do for my child, and I haven't even met them yet.

I will fight, live, move Heaven and Earth to protect that child. I won't stop until I'm back with Ashton and can see everything is all right.

She and that baby are why I'm working as hard as I am to get through to him. I'm going to use his family as a common ground, maybe if he can see that I'm going to be a father too, he'll snap out of whatever this shit is.

"Aarabelle loves him more."

"That's not true, Aaron. You're her father. She loves you."

He scoffs. "She's why I'm gone! I can't be this monster in front of her! I can't let her see how fucking broken and damaged I am. Don't you see, Quinn, we're the same. We were injured, beaten down, and then we thought we could come back and it would be like it was. It's never the same!"

If he didn't have me ripped from my life, I would feel bad for him. He's clearly fucked in the head from all that happened. This isn't a man trying to go out for vengeance, he's just lost.

"So, you're protecting her from you?"

"Someone has to."

The shame and devastation in his voice staggers me. Then I think about the conversations I had with Mark about his location. They seemed to believe he was fine. He's clearly not.

"Aaron, where does everyone think you are?"

He jerks his head to the door, and I listen for whatever noise caught his attention. I pray to God that whoever showed up is on my side and not his. I know I never would've guessed this shit, but . . . maybe.

I wrestle to my feet as quietly as I can, ready to help in any way if it means I can get the fuck out of here.

Aaron turns, and his face is contrite as he punches me in the stomach and slips the bag over my head a second before the dark isn't from the lack of light.

Fuck. I've been drugged again.

I have to get out of here.

The only thing preventing it is the fact that he keeps fucking drugging me. It's hard to plan an escape when you're passed out.

So, I'm lying here in this dirty room that I've been in for God knows how long, doing everything in my power to be completely motionless.

I know I'm in a warehouse. I'm fairly certain I'm in the New York area. There are sounds and smells that I've grown accustomed to since being here with Ashton.

Ashton.

No—stop it. I can't let myself go down that road. It will only make me desperate, and impatience isn't something I can afford.

I have to keep my head on straight, which means not thinking about her even though she's the reason I *am* going to get the hell out of here.

"What are you planning to do with him?"

Aaron's voice is distant but clear. "I'm going to talk some sense into him. If I can make him see what a mistake he's making, then I'll have saved one from their clutches."

"And if he doesn't cooperate?"

"He will," Aaron says.

I'm still completely baffled that it's him behind this. He was one of Jackson's best friends. I know he's been through hell, but this is a whole new level of betrayal. Then I wonder what exactly Mark and Jackson think Aaron is doing. And what about Natalie and Liam? Neither of them has said a goddamn word about him.

It is as if he was there and then gone.

"I still think this is a stupid plan," the guy says.

"You were in the same war as I was. You saw the same shit. You know what it all means! I can't . . . let this happen again."

They move around, and I hear a chair scrape. "If anyone finds out it's us . . ."

"You think I'm stupid? I know this group. Cole is predictable. Dixon is emotional. Dempsey is a coward. Each one of those guys will fail because I know their weaknesses."

"Okay, and what about this guy?"

"He's bait."

He's fucking deranged. That much is clear. I try to think like a lunatic for a minute. If I wanted to get back at someone, I would lure them out and then get their guards down, which is exactly what will happen when they realize it's Aaron.

He's their friend.

They clearly care about him, otherwise, they would've told me about whatever the hell is going on. Instead, they protected him.

I hear my door crank open. They both fall quiet, and I stay extra still. If they think I'm still out, there's a likelihood they'll keep talking.

"So, he was your friend?"

"They all were," Aaron replies. "Until they left me to fucking rot, stole my wife, my kid, and my life . . . so, it's time to repay the favor."

I have to hope they won't make the same mistake they made with Aaron and not let me fucking rot. Otherwise, the bait will become chum.

chapter six

ASHTON

"**A**ARON, AS IN, AARON AND NATALIE?"
Jackson looks down at his phone again as though it's some kind of calculus question he's stuck on. "Yes. That's what the photo shows."

"Where the fuck has he been?" I ask with a bite in my voice that is almost murderous.

Aaron is a goddamn SEAL like them. He works for Jackson. He's *friends* with Jackson and Mark. This is the most ridiculous thing I've ever heard.

Gretchen squeezes my shoulders. "After I uncovered some of the issues with Jackson's legal team, I started to dig deeper. Typically, if you find something on the surface then chances are more is buried. The deeper I looked, the more I found, but I couldn't really make sense of it. A lot of the stuff Aaron oversaw, but he didn't remember any of it."

Jackson nods. "He was having periods where it seemed he blacked out or had no memories. He talked about the dreams he was having, and all of us knew something was really wrong."

"So, he went insane?" I ask. "And no one thought to tell anyone?"

Mark returns to our little party. "He checked out or signed out or something, but he's been gone about two weeks now."

I huff. "You guys are kidding me, right? You had him committed?"

"No," Jackson answers. "We got him help at one of the best facilities for PTSD and other combat issues."

I shake my head in disbelief. "If this is true, and that's Aaron in that photo, what does it mean?"

That's the man I love in there, and he's been taken by one of their friends. Aaron has way more history with these guys than Quinn does. They weren't on the same team, fighting side by side like Aaron, Jackson, and Mark were. There's history there, and I'm not at all okay with how the odds are silently stacking in my head.

Quinn is my concern.

Not some brotherly bond. I don't care if that makes me a bitch. I've lost enough, and I'm not willing to lose anything else.

"It means we have to be even more cautious."

"Cautious how?"

Mark takes my hand in his. "It means we have to worry about everything. He knows us. He knows what we'd do in this situation. He'll have contingency plans for all the possibilities because Aaron literally wrote our combat handbooks. Not to mention, he's our friend and has been in actual combat with us, so he will know exactly how we will handle something like this. We have to take a beat, collect ourselves, and rethink things."

I want to say more, but Gretchen speaks first. "I think what she's worried about is Quinn's safety in all this."

"He's our first concern," Jackson says quickly. "Make no mistake, we will go get him and we'll do whatever we have to secure his safety."

Mark jumps in. "We just have to also prepare for the fact that our enemy is also a friend."

My apartment has become overcrowded in the last twenty-four hours. Men of all kinds of military or police occupations have come to give advice.

I stopped listening about thirty minutes ago when they were talking about the hostage and angles of gunfire. It's too much for me.

I came into my bedroom, turned the television on, and have been ignoring it all since.

They plan, they unplan, they plan some more, and no one does shit. If I could walk faster, I would've already gone and rescued him.

A soft knock raps on the door and then it opens. Charlie, Mark's wife, gives a soft smile. "May I come in?"

"Do you promise not to feed me bullshit?"

She chuckles once. "I don't even know how to."

That is why I like her. "Come in then."

"How are you doing?"

I watch her, wondering how much she wants me to say. The polite thing would be something to make her feel like she tried and it's appreciated. The thing is, Charlie doesn't care about any of that. She's in the trenches and deals with far worse than anything I could say.

"I'm miserable."

She nods. "Sounds about right. I'm glad you didn't tell me you were good. I would've laughed at you."

At least I read that right. "Anything new?"

Charlie moves toward the bed, pulling the chair over with her. "Yes and no. It's definitely Aaron, which is the worst news for the guys, but I think it's actually a good thing. No matter what Aaron's state of mind is, those guys are the last people he'll want to hurt. I'm trying to give them all the alternate sides of it so they're informed."

"You don't seem nervous."

"I'm not. I know Mark and Jackson, they won't fail."

I play with a string on my blanket. "We all have different definitions of failure."

Charlie's voice softens a bit. "Yes, and we all have crosses to bear from our decisions. They're struggling with all of it and trying to make the best contingencies . . . while they pretend they're not drowning in guilt and grief."

"Because Aaron's their friend?" I ask.

She shakes her head. "No, because you are. Mark looks at you and sees the situation as if it were me sitting in this room going out of my mind. Jackson sees Catherine. It's a horrible thing to love someone and know that your choice is what caused their misery. I'm not saying this because *you* have any reason to feel bad, but there's enough blame, emotions, sadness, and whatever else we can shovel onto this situation."

This part confuses me. "What are they upset about?"

Her eyes narrow a little as she tilts her head. "You don't see it?"

"See what?"

"They love you, Ashton. They are devastated by all you've been through and that the one thing they want—to get Quinn back for you—could come at a personal cost to them. You're part of their family, and to see you struggle is beyond words for those guys."

I didn't think they were stressed because of me. "I love them too."

"I know that, and so do they, which makes it that much harder for them. Mark was . . ." Charlie seems a million miles away for a second "He was a lot of things the day you lost the baby. He couldn't find Quinn. He couldn't get to you. He couldn't get anything to work. I haven't seen him that upset in a very long time."

"You know, this is the first time anyone has talked to me about it without trying to make me feel better." There's no judgment between us. She's okay with what I say and vice versa. Charlie is laying out the facts and also helping me see that this is hard on everyone. I knew it wasn't easy, but I didn't think about how it might be for them.

I'm still so deeply in pain that I haven't looked outside myself very much at all.

"Whenever things get strained for me, I hate when other people try to get me to . . . *see*." She makes air quotes around that word. "I see what I want and telling me to open my eyes doesn't do anything but piss me off. All I can do is present the truth as I see it."

"I hate that any of them think that way."

Charlie smiles with a hint of sadness. "I'm glad you still care about them. I know they're dumb and this whole thing has been beyond unbearable for you, but they're trying. I promise. I don't think Aaron is a bad guy, I think he's just lost."

I think back to a distant memory. "You were who got Aaron out of there, weren't you?"

"I was."

"And did you think he was capable of this?"

She looks off and shrugs. "I think people are capable of unthinkable things. I look at some of the criminals and terrorists I've come in contact with over the years. They were fathers, husbands, sons, daughters, or mothers, and something happened to alter the course of their beliefs. Things we can't rationalize because there's nothing rational about what they're doing. Like I said, I don't think he's himself right now, though. I know all of what is going on and how much the guys are worried about him. We all thought he was getting help."

I want to have empathy, but I don't. He did this. It's his fault this is happening, so fuck him and the help he needs. He caused this hurt, and he'll have to suffer for it. If anyone expects *me* to feel bad, they can fuck right the hell off with him.

"What do we do now?"

"I wish I knew," Charlie says honestly. "He could be angry with the guys, and that's why he's doing this. If that's the case, then Mark, Liam, and Jackson going in could exacerbate the situation. If it's something else, they could calm him enough to extract Quinn. Do you see why they're not moving quickly?"

I do, but it doesn't change the fact that Quinn is the one suffering from all of this. The more time we waste, the higher the possibility of my losing him forever becomes. I'm not an expert on all of this like they are, but even I know that time is everything.

"And at what point do we put Quinn's needs ahead of Aaron's?"

Charlie masks any reaction a normal person might have had. "That's exactly what they're doing."

I lean back, tired from all of it. "Then I hope Aaron doesn't have needs we're not thinking of."

chapter seven

QUINN

ARON WALKS IN CARRYING FOOD. I DON'T TRUST ANYTHING from him, but I'm starving. I held off eating the last twenty-four hours because the drugs he gave me are killing my stomach.

Still, he tries to get me to eat.

"I'm not poisoning you," he says as though he can read my mind.

"I appreciate that, but can you blame me for being apprehensive?"

He is one of us. He is my brother in arms. I would do anything for him, even now. Once a SEAL, always a SEAL. There's a code and family tie that's unbreakable. This, however, crosses the line.

You don't kidnap your friends.

"You know me."

"I don't right now."

Aaron places the tray down. "I'm the same guy, just tired of allowing life to happen to me."

"So, you decided to what?"

It's clear that he's having some kind of mental break and

suffering from PTSD. He's erratic, confused, and angry one minute and then thinks we're friends the next. There's nothing I can
say to make sense of it, but if I can understand him, it may allow
me to manipulate him.

"Everything was fine, you know? I was okay with Lee and
Liam. I loved her enough to want her to be happy. And then
I couldn't handle it. She'd come to work, smiling, and I knew
that . . . I should've fucking died. If I hadn't come back, then I
would've never known about it. I wouldn't have had to watch
her be happy, raising *my* child, loving *my* best friend."

Jesus. "You're still in love with her?"

"No. I'm not. I don't want to be with her, but I want my
fucking life back. I want the dreams to stop. I want to stop
walking around wondering if someone is hiding around every
corner."

So many guys come home fucked up from war. Many are
too proud to get help. Some don't think it's an issue or that they
can handle it. I'll never know what it was like for him. He was
held captive for a long time and by people who weren't worried
about his food.

He went days without eating and months without any com-
munication. It took Charlie figuring out who he was for him to
be extracted.

What he endured makes me want to go there and kill them,
but then I remember that he's doing the same thing to me.

Maybe that's the angle I need to play at.

"Then why are you doing that now?"

"Doing what?"

"This," I say as I look around the room he has me in. "You've
got me locked up like you were. I don't get it, man. We're friends,
or at least I thought we were."

He moves closer. "We are friends. I'm not doing this to

punish anyone. I can't sit back and watch it happen again. It starts as a mission and then ends with your entire life being gone like that!" His hands slam together, making a loud *clap*.

As he's been talking, I've been working at getting my hands free. While the last thing I want to do is hurt him, I'm done.

I can't fight him when I'm knocked out, but I can now.

This is the first opportunity that has arisen where I have him alone and unguarded.

"What makes you think that Ashton is going to run off with someone else or that I'm going to get hurt?"

Aaron scoffs. "Look at everyone. Name one guy who hasn't ended up in trouble."

"That's who we are," I remind him.

We're warriors and we fight. When you're in a war, casualties and injuries will happen, it's unavoidable, but we're not at war now and this isn't my fight.

"No, that's just it." His voice becomes animated. "There's this whole other world where we don't have to be shot or killed. We can raise families, have normal lives. I want that, Quinn, but it's too late for me. It's not for you, though."

"I'm going to raise a family and have the life I want, Aaron. This, though? This isn't what I want."

He gets to his feet, and his eyes fill with rage. "You don't know what you want. I'm going to show you how wrong you are. You see, this is a long game. It's not just about you. It's about all of us. Once the team figures out it's me, they'll come, and then I'll finally be able to breathe, because it'll be over."

"You said this wasn't about revenge."

"It's not. It's about justice. Everyone needs to see the errors we made. It all started when we signed up. We were promised the navy would take care of us, but they didn't. They sent us into a war without any idea of what was to come. Then we trusted

Jackson." He sneers his name. "I gave my life to him and he left me there to rot. I'm giving you the chance here, Quinn. Choose right because you don't know what you're giving up."

Aaron apparently missed the training part of our lives. "I knew what I was signing up for."

"This?" he screams. "Was this what you thought it would be?"

I shake my head with a laugh as I try not to lunge at him. There's no way I can anyway. I don't know where I am or what traps he's laid out. It's clear that he's thought this through, and he would expect me to do that. I need to be patient, wait him out, keep him talking to give me more slip-ups.

"No, I guess I didn't think that my friend would fucking abduct me, keep me locked in a room, drug me, and hit me," I spit back at him.

Aaron goes to say something, but there's a loud *bang* and dust fills the room as the door comes flying off the hinges. I scramble to my feet, trying to get out of the way. I'm tired, and my legs are like jelly, but I keep myself upright. When I look over, Mark and Jackson are standing there. Their guns are raised, pointed at Aaron and he grins.

"Took you boys long enough." Aaron heads my way, getting closer even though their muzzles are trained on him.

Jackson's gaze doesn't waver from Aaron, and Mark takes a step toward me. "Aaron, move away from Quinn."

"Or what? You're going to shoot me, brother?"

Adrenaline fills my body, giving me back the strength that's been stolen from me. I watch for their cues. Anything to tell me the next play. Mark moves his head side to side just enough to tell me to stay put.

"It's not what either of us wants."

"I didn't want any of this!" Aaron bellows.

Mark takes another step. "Neither do we, but we're not going to let you hurt Quinn."

"And I'm not going to let you hurt him either. I won't let you destroy him like you destroyed *me*!"

The two of them don't flinch, but anyone would be a fool to think that didn't hurt.

Jackson moves to the right. "Then we're all in agreement that this needs to end. We all know you're not a cold-hearted killer. Whatever this is it has to do with what we all talked about a few months ago."

When Aaron laughs, so much anger fills the room that I would cower if I were less of a man.

Then Liam steps through the door. "It's me you're angry at, isn't it?"

Something in Aaron shifts. I can't explain it, but his entire demeanor changes when he sees him.

Liam starts again. "You see it as if I've taken everything from you."

"No."

"No? Because that's what you told your friend out there. That your best friend took your life when you died."

My heart is pounding, and I can taste the mixed emotions in the room. This is a disaster waiting to happen. Aaron left his gun on the ground by the tray of food over to the right. If I could grab it, I could shoot him in the leg. As pissed off as I am that I'm here, the truth is that I don't want to see him dead. I want to get to Ashton.

Now that I've allowed myself to think of her, my impatience grows. I look over to the left, hoping Mark will catch my gaze. He starts talking. "We all know that Liam didn't take anything. You've suffered horribly, and we don't want to see you hurt more."

"Which is why my three best friends have guns pointed at me? Go ahead . . . I dare you to shoot me. You can't fucking do it."

Liam moves closer, he releases his hold on the gun, one hand going up in the air as the other, holding the gun lowers. "I'm not going to shoot you," he says with a calm voice. "I can't do it. You're right."

I move again, closer now to the gun, but my energy is waning. I'm fucking tired. I've been through hell in these last God only knows how many days. There's practically nothing left inside me. The will to fight is there, but that's only for her.

Then everything flashes in a second. "Well, I can." Aaron reaches behind him, revealing a gun in his belt, and I lunge for the gun on the floor as the sound of a bullet exiting the chamber echoes through the room.

chapter eight

ASHTON

"WHAT WAS THAT? GUNSHOTS?" I SCREAM AND MOVE TO head into the warehouse. Two sets of arms wrap around my shoulders, stopping me.

"Ashton, stop," Ben commands. "You can't go in there. Not only because we have no idea what is going on but also because it would be dangerous and a distraction."

I start to tremble. I had to beg, plead, promise the moon to even get to come here, but I won Jackson and Mark over. There was not a chance in hell I wasn't going, and I think they knew that. If he's hurt, I need to see to him. If he's dead, I want to know. If he's fine, I have to touch his face, his heart, and then break it.

Charlie pulls me toward the car. "Come on, let's sit and wait."

"How can you be so calm? Your husband is in there!"

She nods. "Yes, and I trust him. He's smart, and he's good at what he does."

I wish I could be so confident. My nerves are frayed, and I still have so much more to wade through. When Quinn is out and safe, I'll have to tell him everything. I can't run into his arms, kissing his lips, and be grateful he's alive. I can barely walk, and thanks to my outburst, I'm in pain again.

My head is filled with so many possibilities that it starts to ache. "I'm scared," I admit.

Not only of whatever is happening but also of what's to come.

Charlie's eyes go from the door back to me. "I can't imagine what you're feeling, Ashton, but I hope you hear me when I say that you've been through a trauma, just like Quinn has. We often forget that and try to be strong and act as though these situations haven't shaped us in some way, but they do. They change us. Don't let it take over, though. You're both going to need each other."

Ben raises his hand, and Charlie rushes over. I want to go, but I feel as though my incision is on fire. Slowly, I get myself to standing as the two of them talk. She heads back to me. "Come on, they're coming out."

"Alive?"

"I don't know."

The urge to cry is threatening to overtake me, but I hold back. I can't fall apart. He needs me to be strong, and this isn't the time for me to lose it. That part will come, and I am dreading it ever so much.

Jackson emerges first, his eyes are unreadable from this distance, but his posture is loose, almost relaxed. He stops and turns back toward the building as Liam exits, holding someone who appears to be limping. Jackson's other arm wraps around the man's torso, and I realize it's Aaron.

I start to walk, forcing myself to ignore the pain. I just move. Quinn is somewhere. He's either hurt or dead or perfectly fine, and no matter what, I need him. My pulse is racing as I keep moving, not hearing or concentrating on anything going on around me.

My focus is only on what could be behind that steel door.

It flies open.

I stop moving, waiting, as my legs feel like they could give out. Then I see him.

His eyes are dark, his skin is dirty, and he's still wearing the same clothes he left in that day. Mark holds him up, and then his gaze meets mine.

Quinn pushes Mark off and starts toward me, but in some recess of my brain, I remember to control myself, and I don't move. As soon as he's within my grasp, my hands move to his face. My God, he's alive. He's here, and I can touch him.

"*Fragolina*," he says as a prayer. Never before has his voice sounded so perfect.

I touch his cheeks, moving my thumb across the bones below his eyes. "I didn't think I'd ever see you again," I say the words with tears falling.

"I'm too much of a bastard to die."

A half-laugh that turns into a sob escapes my throat. "I'm glad for it." My hand continues to touch his face, his neck, his shoulders. "Are you hurt?"

"No, sweetheart, I'm okay."

"The gunshots?"

Quinn turns to look at Aaron, but I pull his face back to me. I don't want to go without seeing his eyes. "He got a shot off, but I was able to do what those three didn't want to do."

"You shot him?" I ask.

"I have really good aim and incapacitated him." His dirty hands cup my face, wiping away the tears. "Are you okay?"

This is where I should tell him, but it isn't the right time. I want to feel him, touch him, stay in this little slice of happiness before it's gone. We'll have to mourn our loss, live it all over again. I'm not ready.

Time is what we need.

Only we're short on it. "Can we get you checked out before we talk about everything that's happened?" I ask, hoping that he'll give me just a sliver of what I ask.

"Are you okay?"

I nod. "I am now."

He brings his lips to mine, giving me the sweetest kiss that is filled with his relief and flavored with tears.

When he pulls back, Quinn searches my eyes. "Then let's get checked out so I can take a shower. Then I need you to reassure me that I haven't lost you."

I pull his mouth back to mine. "You haven't." *But we've lost our child.* I think to myself, hating the words as a new round of tears fall.

Quinn doesn't require three nights of a hospital stay. Instead, they checked him over, did bloodwork, and gave him an IV because he was dehydrated. Now we're on our way home. There was a constant stream of people, which allowed us zero time to talk. I can't even hope that there would be chaos in my apartment to act as a distraction because the boys assured me they would be cleared out and everything would be back to normal by the time we got back.

We sit in the back of the cab, holding each other's hands, the tension mounting as we near my apartment.

I pay the cabbie, and we exit, still not speaking. The quiet is the calm before the explosion. There's no doubt he knows it too. What will be the cause of detonation? I wonder. Will it be me because I'm brimming with the need to say it? Will it be him?

Then I wonder if he already knows. Quinn is overly

observant. He sees things that others miss, and maybe my si-lence is telling him all the words I don't want to speak aloud.

After all the activity today, I'm in excruciating pain. My inci-sion, which was burning before, has become an inferno. We get upstairs, and when we cross the threshold to the door, I almost double over.

"Ashton!" Quinn yells as his arm grips me.

I look up, tears fill my gaze, blurring his face. The only way I'm going to get it out is if I don't see his eyes. The nausea as-saults me, and I blurt the words, knowing there is no amount of finesse that will make this blow any easier. "I lost the baby. I hope you'll forgive me but, it's gone."

His other hand wraps around my back, and he pulls me to his chest. "No."

I can see the pain in his gaze as he stares at me. His lip quiv-ers just a bit, but he shoves it down, trying to be strong.

Here was what I dreaded, the pain and sadness of losing something that we created. Just like I'm going to lose him.

"I'm so sorry!" I say as the tears fall. "I'm . . . I'm just . . ."

His hand rests on the back of my head. "No, I'm sorry I wasn't here for you."

I start to sob and let the weight of everything press me closer to him. It's as though I found out all over again. I want to tear my heart out because it hurts too much in my chest. All of what we had is gone.

Quinn walks me to the couch, never letting go of me. I cry so hard that I worry I'll tear a staple. He doesn't say anything, he holds me close, allowing me to release it all.

The pain.

The fear.

The sadness.

The anger because I'm so fucking angry.

"I lo-lost the baby, Quinn. I l-lost our b-baby." My teeth rattle as I shake with agony. "I couldn't s-stop it!"

"Don't cry, Ashton. You didn't do anything."

No, I didn't *do* anything. I just let it happen because I'm sure I forgot something important and that's why it happened. I didn't eat right. I forgot my prenatal vitamins once or twice, too. My clothes were too tight or maybe it was the trip to the beach where we walked too much. There's a reason somewhere. I know there is.

These things happen, but there's *always* something that causes it.

It was clearly because of me.

I don't know for sure, and I won't likely ever find out.

"I did nothing but cry and wish I had died along with her. What kind of mother would I have been anyway?"

"Her?" he asks. "Do you know?"

I shake my head. "I don't want to know, but I . . . I couldn't ask. I can't . . . I . . . I took her away."

"You didn't do anything wrong! You didn't take her away or decide to lose the baby, Ashton."

I wipe away the tears I don't deserve to cry. Fuck it. I'm angry now. "I was supposed to protect her! It was my only job!"

He cups my cheeks gently, forcing me to look at him. "Stop it. Stop it right now! You didn't do this. You loved that baby, and there was no way you did anything on purpose."

I wish I could believe him. "You weren't there!" I get to my feet as a new wave of agony rips through me. "You didn't see! You didn't . . . you couldn't . . . and then you were gone. I lost everything! Everything!" The last word cracks in a mix of sorrow and anger.

He pulls me back down, holding me tightly, his arms acting as a shield against the pain, and I smother my face in his chest. I want to go to sleep and never wake up to live in this nightmare. It's all too much.

"I should've been there. I wanted to get to you, and I hate myself for letting you down."

"You were . . . God, Quinn, you were taken!"

He pushes my hair back off my wet cheeks. "I should've fought to escape, but I wasn't sure how it would play out. I had to be smart, and all this time you were here suffering."

There's so much guilt cocooning us that one of us may suffocate under it. He kisses the top of my head, letting me lose myself as I will my tears away. I've cried enough, and I don't deserve to release it.

"You say you don't blame me, so what makes you think I blame you?"

"Because I would. I never should've followed him. You told me you needed me, and I thought I could wait another two minutes, get the info, and get back here. I was a fool."

No, he isn't a fool. He was doing his job while I was failing to do mine. I'm angry, sad, overwhelmed, happy he's alive, angry again that we had to go through this. It doesn't make any sense, and there's nothing that will ever fix it.

"You didn't lose our child, Quinn. You didn't—" *lose the only chance we'll ever have.* I can't say the last part because it will be where he sees how I'm no longer whole. Instead, I give him the out he deserves. "I understand if you want to leave."

Quinn pulls back and forces my eyes to meet his. "Leave?"

"I promised you something that I can't give."

His head tilts to the side as though he's trying to figure out what I'm saying. "What did you promise?"

"A life. A baby. My heart. I don't care, take your pick. I can't give you any of those right now."

"Ashton, I love you, and I'm . . . heartbroken that we lost the baby. I would've given anything to . . . but . . . it's *you* who is my life and my heart. The entire time I was gone, all I did was try to hold on to the fact that I had to live to get back to you. I had to force myself not to think of your face." He runs his hand along my cheek. "Your eyes." Quinn touches the skin below, running along the dark circles there. "Or dream about your smile and your heart or I would've never made it out of there. I was always told that loving someone made you weak, and they were wrong, sweetheart. So wrong. I wasn't weak because of loving you, I was strong and determined, even when I felt beaten. You were what made me live. We have a long future ahead of us and time for a baby. I'm not leaving you. I lived to get back to you."

I shake my head as he's about to find out that I'm not just broken, I'm destroyed. "There will never be a baby for us, Quinn."

"I know you're hurting, and I'm not asking for you to try anytime soon . . ."

I push back out of his arms, but my hand stays on his chest so he doesn't come closer. "No. I'm saying that we will never have a child. I will never have a child."

"I don't understand," his voice is filled with apprehension.

"I didn't just lose the baby, I lost everything. I'm unable to have a child. Ever."

chapter nine

ASHTON

*N*OT A SINGLE TEAR FILLS MY GAZE AS I WATCH HIS FACE. I wait for a reaction, but Quinn is a trained man. He doesn't flinch or change his posture. He looks at me with studying eyes, and slowly, the man emerges.

He shakes his head in disbelief, expression filling with sadness. "I don't understand. You don't want to try again?"

My heart lurches because there's nothing I want more. I would give it all back—him, my job, my home, my entire life—if it meant that I could try again. "It wasn't just a miscarriage, Quinn. I lost everything. I had to have a—" I hiccup and lock up my emotions because I need to say it. "Hysterectomy. There was too much bleeding, and to save my life . . . well, we can never have children—or, at least, I can never have children."

The words seep in, I watch as awareness that it wasn't a tragic miscarriage starts to settle over him. It was the end of the dreams I once had.

The family I envisioned with him. The little girls with my red hair and his smile are gone. The boy that had his strong jaw, dark brown hair, and my eyes fade like mist in the morning, evaporating with the sun that I wish never came. In the light, there is truth that only the darkness hides. There's no more darkness here.

"I failed you." Quinn's voice snaps me out of my daze.

"You what?"

Doesn't he understand it wasn't him? He did nothing wrong. I did it all. I'm the one who should be getting yelled at because I'm responsible for all of this. Only he doesn't see it, which is the worst part of it all. He'll wake up one day, looking at me with the same hatred in which I look at myself. He'll know that it was me who caused this level of grief for our could-be family.

I know what it feels like to be let down by someone you love.

It eats at you and allows resentment to fester.

When Quinn speaks, his voice is layered with hurt. "I wasn't here. I should've run right here, to you. You went through all of this alone? You honestly thought I would be angry with you, Ashton?"

My breaths come out in small puffs, as though my lungs are afraid to pull the air because I might choke on it. "I don't know. I didn't know what you'd be because I'm livid! I'm livid and hurt and broken and so much more. You should be angry at me!"

Quinn shifts forward, his hands move to my shoulders before drifting to my neck and then my face. "I'm not angry at you, *fragolina*. I'm angry at *myself*."

"You didn't take her from us."

"You mean that I wasn't here to support you when you were losing something precious to us."

I close my eyes, blocking the comfort he's offering. He can't say these things to me. Being understanding now will only make it all worse later. "You're in shock. You've been through hell and—"

"And you haven't?" His voice is soft. "You don't think that

what you've endured this last week wasn't horrific? Losing the baby, not knowing what was happening to me, finding out that you couldn't . . ."

"Say it," I taunt him.

"Why? Why does it matter? Why do you want me to hurt you?"

Then the tears fall. The fucking truth of the hurt I'm trying to hide. This is where I can't seem to control myself. He can't hurt me any more than I already am. "I lost everything!" I scream. "I have . . . nothing inside me anymore, Quinn! Don't you get it? I'm not even a woman! I'm . . . I'm hollow and ruined." I sniff and move away from him. "Hurt me? *Please*. You can't hurt what's already dead inside."

The determination in his eyes causes me to step back. "Are you hearing yourself? You're not dead inside. If you were, when I exited that warehouse, you wouldn't have cared. You would've been emotionless. Hell, you probably wouldn't even have been there in the first place. I've seen dead inside, sweetheart. I've watched men who were full of life reduced to nothing. That's not you. It's not what will ever become of you."

How I wish that were true. "I allowed myself emotion, some small semblance of it when you were missing because I was so afraid, but you're here now."

"How does that change anything?" Quinn asks.

Because I don't have to try anymore. I can finally allow myself to go to that quiet, sorrow-filled place and stay there. He can't even begin to fathom the level of grief that's been crushing me, inching nearer with each breath. I can't hold it back any longer. There's not enough strength in my body to fight.

"I'm not strong enough," I admit.

Quinn brings his lips to mine. "I'm strong enough for the both of us, Ashton. I won't let you fall apart."

He's too late, and I'm too tired. I don't admit that because I'm smart enough to know that he won't listen. He'll try to convince me that I'm wrong, but his words won't heal the damage my body has caused.

After I get most of my tears out, Quinn carries me to the bedroom. He's exhausted, I'm emotional, and we're both out of words.

His breathing is steady as my head rests in the crook of his arm. I look at him, watching the way his eyelids move slightly as he finally rests. I wonder how long it will be until I'm staring at the empty pillow. Will it take him weeks to accept what I am? Months? If I know Quinn, he'll try for a period of time, but he'll eventually go.

He never dreamed of a family. He didn't see the children, love, and life we could have until I put it in his head—the fairy tale that will never be.

There are many women who don't have children and are perfectly happy, but I will never be one of them. I wanted to be a mother more than anything else in the world and was willing to go at it on my own if that was what I needed to do.

Now, not even that is an option.

What a cruel twist of fate.

In his sleep, he pulls me closer, almost as if he knows I'm drifting in my own depression.

"Sleep, Ash," his voice is a whisper.

"I can't."

He shifts to his side. The dim light of dawn is starting to break through the windows, but it's enough for me to be able to see his face. "I can feel you thinking."

It's all I do. I think, wish, curse everything, and think more. I can't stop my mind from going through it over and over. I see that day play out like a movie stuck on the same scene. The blood when I stood from the couch. The way I knew that something was wrong. Clara's voice when I called. The face of the cabbie as he drove me into the city.

Then the relief I allowed myself to feel.

I remember the split second when I saw that I wasn't bleeding as I exited the car. I thought that maybe I was overreacting. I hoped that it was a sign that I was going to be all right.

And then . . . the pain as I walked through that door.

The sensation of something tearing me open and then the blood.

His thumb brushes my cheek. "Ashton?"

"I see it play out every time I close my eyes. If I had . . . done anything different, would it have mattered?"

"Given everything you know, could you have prevented it?" There is no trace of judgment in his voice.

No. "That's the worst part, there isn't."

"Then why do you think you could've stopped it?"

I release a heavy sigh and shift to my back, being careful because I'm very sore. "Because my mother has always said there's nothing like the strength of a mother's love. I'm going to sleep now," I say the last part and close my eyes. Clearly, my love wasn't strong enough.

"You've been doing too much," Clara says as she looks over my incision. "You pulled a staple and it looks like you could have an infection in the incision. I'm going to put you on some antibiotics and demand that you take it easy. You had major surgery ten days ago, and you need to start acting like it so you can heal."

Quinn moves to my side, taking my hand. "I'm trying to get her to rest, but she's having a hard time sleeping and getting comfortable. For the last three days, she's been restless and uncomfortable."

Clara's eyes meet mine before moving to Quinn. "Can you step out for a few? I'd like to speak with Ashton for a bit."

I nod, letting him know it's okay.

"Sure, Dr. Madison."

"Please call me Clara," she insists.

"Clara, then. I'll be right outside, Ash . . . if you need me."

The last seventy-two hours have been hell for us. I feel as though we've run a marathon and haven't come close to the end yet. We talk but I always end up zoning out. He tries to engage me, I move further away. It's just . . . the only way I can protect myself against when he finally sees the truth of all that happened. Quinn does everything he can to ease my mind, but it's not that simple.

"Ashton, how are you really?"

I shrug. "I'm here."

"Are you?"

"I don't know," I admit. I'm here physically, but my heart is gone.

"You know, all of this is normal," Clara says. "It would be good to talk to someone. We have Sarina on staff, and she's a fantastic psychologist. She's dealt with this many times."

I'm sure all of that is true. Sarina is great, but there's no point in talking. "It doesn't change the facts."

"No, but it could change your emotions about the facts."

"How would you feel?" I toss back at her and then look away.

"I'd be angry."

I laugh without humor. "Well, I'm fucking enraged."

Clara expels a breath through her nose and watches me. "I can see that. So, you're ranging from the stages of isolation and anger?"

"Fuck all of you, Clara. You think I want this? I got Quinn back from the clutches of his insane friend to have to tell him I lost our child. So, am I angry? You're damn right I am. Am I isolating myself? Sure. What the hell is the point to any of this? What good does talking do? Does it bring back my baby? Does it make me whole again? Nope. So, I don't want to talk to Sarina or any other doctor who is going to tell me how what I'm going through is normal. Nothing is normal. I'm fucking done."

Clara's eyes are wide, but there's also a bit of arrogance there. She played me, and I strolled right into it. "I think you're definitely in the anger stage, my friend. Good thing I've dealt with shit much scarier than you or that little tirade *might* have made me cry."

I shake my head and look away. I shouldn't have snapped at her. She's only trying to help. "I'm sorry. I'm overtired, and I'm—it's been a lot."

Clara nods. "It has been, that's why I think it would be good to get some help."

"I appreciate it, Clara. I need to find a new normal without anyone else trying to analyze my feelings. I'll get there, but it's going to take more than two weeks to get over losing her."

"Her?"

My chest grows tight because Clara would know. She would've had to document whether the baby was a boy or a girl.

"I meant, the child."

"Do you need answers?" Her tone is careful and my heart lurches.

Do I? Can I handle it? What would it change? In my mind,

I am allowed the disillusions of what she was. I'm allowed to live the lie I've created to protect myself in my misery. Knowing changes nothing and will only make the baby real. I would want to name her, give her a permanent place in this world. Even though she never drew a breath, she was ours.

"No. No, I'd rather not know. I don't ever want to think about this. I don't want to talk to anyone. I have no plans to delve into my damn emotions because I have none, so please, let me go and grieve the way I need to."

Clara is a good friend who I hope understands not to push me on this. It's not that I'm opposed to therapy, but I'm too deep in my own emotions to even consider talking about them. How do you make someone who has spent their entire adult life creating babies accept that they're not able to do it for themselves? You can't. No one can help me through it.

Sarina is a great therapist, and I've seen her help many people in our facility, but I won't be one of them.

Once I'm on my own, I'll find a quiet existence in a lab somewhere where I don't have to see people or deal with anything but science.

Science is facts.

Science has definites and solutions.

"Why don't you come back to work in two weeks? You can stay off your feet, go through some of the proposals, and catch up. I know you were going part-time, but I think it could be good for you to come back here."

I look at my colleague and friend, knowing that she's trying to help or give me something to try for. The thing is, I can't ever do this again. I can't stare at an embryo, knowing I'm going to give another woman something so precious that I almost had. I just . . . can't.

"I'm resigning completely."

"What?" There's a mix of sadness and apprehension in her voice. "Ashton, please don't make a decision like that when you're grieving."

"I'm going to be grieving for a long time, Clara. I know what I'm saying."

"And what's going to happen later? What are you going to do?"

"I don't know."

She shakes her head as her warm brown eyes fill with compassion. "You have every right to take some time off if that's what you need, but you have always loved your job."

"I did."

I loved everything about it. It was wonderful knowing that I could be a link in the chain leading toward someone's happiness. My heart would soar when we'd hear of a birth. There was beauty there.

Now, it's tainted.

Maybe I'm being dramatic, but I know I can't stand there and manipulate an egg. I can't watch it grow to an embryo and then see it go into another woman who has all her parts. Not to mention having to watch some of them lose a child and remember my own loss all over again. I'm done.

There's no one that could blame me for feeling this way.

"And do you really think quitting your job is going to make it easier?"

"I can't do this either, Clara. I can't sit here and . . . make babies. Could you? Could you help another woman do something you wanted more than your own life and couldn't? Just the thought of it makes me want to cry, and I'm done crying."

She moves closer, her voice soft and comforting as she says, "You're not close to being done crying, Ash. You haven't begun to scratch the surface of your emotions, and you're going to feel more and less and then more. You're grieving two losses, and you spent the first week of that trying to grapple with Quinn's disappearance. So, in the last ten days, there's no way you've dealt with your grief, never mind had enough time to be in a headspace to make decisions like this."

"You don't have to understand or like it, but I'll be handing in my letter of resignation by tomorrow."

I stand and walk to the door, but then she calls out, "I won't accept it."

My head turns, and I shrug. "You don't have to, but I won't be back."

And with that, I exit the room and pray I never have to walk through these doors again.

chapter ten

QUINN

ASHTON IS A WALKING ZOMBIE. THAT'S THE ONLY WAY I CAN describe it. She's alive, talking and moving, but she's emotionless. Her heart isn't into anything she says or does.

"What did Clara say?" I ask her as we get into the cab.

"Nothing."

"You were in there a long time."

She nods, turning her head to look out the window. "It's Friday, right?"

I don't fucking know. I'm so exhausted and doing my best to wrap my head around everything that I couldn't tell you what month it is. "I honestly couldn't tell you, why?"

Her eyes meet mine, and she shrugs. "It doesn't matter anymore."

I'm racking my brain to figure out where she might have been going with that. I don't think there was anything planned, but I don't pay attention to much of that stuff anyway. The way she said "anymore" leads me to believe it had something to do with the baby.

After a few seconds, it hits me. "Ashton," I say her name softly.

"Yeah?"

"Fridays were when you counted down another week?"

"It's why I said it doesn't matter. I guess I could count the weeks since we lost her."

My heart sinks when I look in her eyes. There's so much pain and sadness. "No, we shouldn't count that."

She laughs without any feelings. "Right, that would be morbid and stupid. We shouldn't. I was joking."

I don't think she was joking at all. I believe she's going to count it in her heart and that each week will drive her further into her grief.

"Okay."

Right now, the ground is covered in razor-sharp eggshells and no matter which way I walk, my feet will bleed. I have a feeling that whatever happened in that room after I left is weighing on her. I can't name why, but she's . . . even more vacant than she was before.

Like something inside her has snapped.

She's not crying or really doing much of anything.

I need my girl to fight. I'm not sure how to elicit that, but I have to try.

We get to the apartment, set our stuff down, and she settles on the couch. I sit beside her, my hand resting on her leg.

"You know that I love you, right?"

Ashton's eyes widen, and she tries for a smile. "Yes."

"Then, will you trust me to talk about what happened in there?"

"In where?"

"In the office with Clara."

Ashton looks away and huffs. "It's nothing. Well, actually I guess it's not nothing, but I should tell you anyway. I quit my job. I figure that, if we're done, I can move back in with my parents until I find something. I'm not sure how you'll feel, so I'm not assuming anything."

My head spins at this revelation. She quit her job without a word to me, which was one of her issues with our relationship before I deployed. That we made big changes without discussing them. I'm not mad that she quit because I don't think she's even remotely thought it through. She loves her job.

"You didn't want to talk to me about it?"

"Why would I? We can be done now, Quinn. I'm not pregnant, so there's no need for you to stick around anymore."

What the hell is she talking about?

"I don't care if you're pregnant, that was never why I came back, and we're not done." She sighs loudly and then shifts, but I grip her wrist before she can get away. "No, we are not done. We're going to talk because I've been trying for months to get this far, and we're sure as fuck not going backward."

"We're not going anywhere. You're okay. I'm alive. We don't have to do this anymore. I know you love me, and I appreciate that you are trying so hard. I really do, but I think it's best if I'm on my own for a while."

I seriously want to throttle her. She thinks I'm going to walk away? Did she not listen to a word I said? "Ashton, I love you. I want to marry you. None of that has changed because we lost our baby."

"No, *I* lost our baby, and it's changed everything."

"I know you're in pain and not thinking clearly."

She shakes her head. "No, that's the thing. I laid in your arms last night and all I could think was: this is all going to end, so why not end it on my terms?"

"So, you're scared?" I ask, and she rips her arm from my grasp.

I may be tired, but there's no way I'm backing down. If

she thinks that I can let this go after all we've been through, she doesn't know me at all.

"No, I'm protecting myself because . . . I can't take anything else. Anything. I can't even fucking breathe! It hurts, Quinn! So, whenever it is that you actually look at this entire situation and wake up from your denial, it won't matter. I will have already saved myself from another round of agony because I won't be there."

There is no way she's leaving me. "Do you think you're the only one who's lost something here? Don't you think I'm in pain at losing her or him? I loved that child just like I love you. With everything I am. So, you don't get to make that choice for me. I love you, and I won't fucking lose you. I didn't live through seven days of absolute hell so that I could come back to you, only to watch you walk away."

Ashton closes her eyes, and her lip trembles before she traps it between her teeth. "Don't do this."

"You don't do this," I plead.

"How long will you stay, Quinn?"

I lift her hand that has the infinity ring I gave her on it and trace the symbol. "For an infinite amount of time."

She scoffs, pulling her hand back. "You say that now, but what about in a year when you realize that I'm not the girl you loved."

"How can you predict who you'll be in a year? And even if you could, how can you not see that it's you. It's always you."

I thought I'd proven that to her. It wasn't the baby or that she could have babies, it is who she is at the core of it all. It's her heart, her fire, and her love. Just the way she looks at me makes me feel whole.

Ashton gets up and walks around the living room, then looks to the ceiling. "If you love me like you say, then you'll end this before I hurt you."

"You ending this is what would hurt," I toss back at her.

The fight seems to drain from her eyes. "You won't love me after a while. You'll resent me when you see how I stole something from you by being selfish."

This is crazy. I walk toward her and grip her shoulders tenderly. "You think that I want kids so badly that I'll leave? I didn't want kids, Ashton, I wanted *our* kids. I never thought about any of that until it was us, and that's what you're failing to see. It isn't about babies or whether you can ever conceive or carry because, without you, I don't give a shit about any of it."

Her eyes fill with tears, and I think that maybe, just maybe, I've gotten through to her. Then she pushes them away, and I watch as the determination consumes the small fraction of emotion she allowed herself.

"Stay if you want, but know that, eventually, your symbol will break and you'll see that I wasn't worth the time you wasted."

I bring my hand to her cheek, moving her hair back as I shake my head. "There's no end for us, Ashton. Start to accept it. If you quit your job and we need to move, then maybe a change of scenery will do us good. We can always go to Virginia Beach."

She shrugs. "That's fine. We can move there, at least I'd have Gretchen."

I kiss her lips, needing her to feel me. "You have me, Ashton."

Her eyes search mine, and I hope she finds what she needs. "I have you . . . for now."

Right now, she's pushing me away, and I understand it, but I vow that I'll bring her back to me, no matter how far she goes.

chapter eleven

ASHTON

"Hi," Cat smiles softly as she and Jackson stand at the front door of the apartment. "We came by to check on you guys before we head to the airport."

I pull it open and step to the side. Quinn is lying down because he's beat and last night he struggled to sleep. I'm not sure I sleep at all anymore. It's more of these moments of half-consciousness, half-unconsciousness. My head moves from thought to thought, never really landing on one solid thing.

"We're doing just fine," I say as they settle their stuff inside, and then my eyes land on Erin in her car seat.

How did I miss it?

Why didn't I think she'd be with them?

My heart lurches, and I hate myself so much for it that I turn away, unable to look at her. I love that baby. She's my niece and goddaughter and I would do anything for her. And yet, I hate that I'll never have one of my own. I want to scream because I'll never have a car seat to carry. I want to throw something, watch it shatter and break until it resembles the broken mess inside me. There was a plan in place that I would have my baby and they'd be best friends. It was all laid out, and I let it fail.

I take a second to gather myself and attempt to smile.

Catherine steps closer, but her gaze doesn't waver, and I swear she can read my mind. "You're not fine."

"No, I guess I'm not."

"I'm going to guess Quinn's not either," she ventures.

"He's better than I am."

Jackson lifts Erin into his arms, cradling her carefully. I watch him protect her without even knowing he's doing it.

"We shouldn't have come," Catherine says with a hint of sadness as she sees the pain spread across my face like a wave. I try to mask it. I do whatever I can to stuff it away because I am going to see babies and children. I'm going to be around people who will get pregnant. Right now, it's as though someone has punched me in the gut.

"I didn't think—"

"No, I'm so sorry. I didn't know Erin would—"

I can't let her think that I didn't want to see Erin. I love her and want to see her. I just . . . I wasn't prepared.

My fingers touch her arm. "Don't say that." Even in all my pain, I don't want my friends to struggle with guilt. They didn't do anything wrong. "It just hurt for a second, but it's not like that."

Catherine gathers me into her arms. "I hate this, Ashton. I hate it, and I don't know how to help you. I love you like a sister, and I would do anything for you."

We embrace each other, but I don't cry. I think I broke my tear ducts because they no longer work. "Well, if you love me so much, maybe you can get me a job," I say as a joke.

She leans back. "What?"

"I quit my job."

"Why? You . . . why the hell would you do that?"

"Because I don't want to help women have babies anymore."

The words are matter of fact and leave no room for arguments. "So, I could open a lab for you guys, and . . . you know . . . I'm sure there are things you need help with that I could arrange. Maybe running DNA tests or something with forensics would be a new venture I could get into?"

Jackson moves closer, and I lock all my emotions down as he approaches. "Are you sure you want to do this? What did Quinn say?"

"He thinks we should move to Virginia Beach, so I'll be looking for a job there once I'm technically cleared to go back to work, I guess."

They share a look, and then Catherine starts. "Ashton, did you really think this through? I'm not saying I don't understand. I do—"

"Do you? Do you know what it's like to be so happy that you're practically dancing on air one day and then in the pits of hell the next?"

Catherine eyes me. "No, but I haven't had the perfect life either, Ashton."

"Have you lost any children?"

"You know I haven't."

"Right, so you totally know what I'm going through. I mean, look, you've had your fair share of shit, but losing not only a baby but also your entire reproductive system seems to tip the scales a bit in my favor."

She huffs. "Jackson, would you give us a minute, please? Maybe Quinn is awake and could use some company."

Damn it. Now she's really going to lay into me. You know what? I don't even care. I'm going to say and feel what the hell I want.

"Sure, I'll go check." He nods once and carries Erin into the back where my bedroom is. I'm being a raging bitch. I know it. As each word escaped my mouth, I hated the way it tasted. Hurting Catherine isn't right, but I'm having a hard time caring much about anything.

"You're right, you know?" she says after he's out of sight. "The scales have tipped so far into the shit side for you that I don't know if there's enough weight to move it back. You didn't deserve any of this, but we're all here for you. We all love you. We all want to help, but for the last week, you've refused to answer phone calls, texts, emails . . . I'm shocked you opened the door."

"I'm tired."

"I get it."

"You say that, but you can't possibly get it. You're able to hold your daughter, love her, touch her . . . I have nothing. So, don't say you get any of it because you have no fucking clue."

"Maybe not," Cat agrees. "Maybe I can't even fathom the kind of hell you're in, but you've never been like this. You're the one who flips the world off as you're strutting by in your Manolo's. You don't sit around and feel sorry for yourself."

"No, that was you," I say and instantly hate myself because that was out of line. "That was . . ."

Catherine didn't deserve that, and I can't seem to make myself say anything.

"True." Catherine shrugs. "I was that way. I let myself fall into despair because it was so much easier. I pushed everyone away, felt as though I didn't deserve anything and almost lost Jackson in the process. Sounds familiar, huh? It was me, but I never thought it would be you."

I didn't get my heart broken by some guy and give up like she did. It has nothing to do with my past or something inconsequential. I lost my life and my future. She has to see there's a difference, and if she doesn't, she's an asshole.

Catherine and I have always had this truth about us, though. She never holds back and neither do I. It's always been full disclosure and maybe I should've expected her to call me out on my reaction. It's that I've never felt this low.

Losing Quinn sucked, and I thought I was pretty pathetic then with how I handled it, but this is more.

This is a heartache I don't understand.

She can judge me, but I know that if the roles were reversed, she'd be no different.

"I never knew what this would feel like."

"You need to let people in. Please, I'm begging you to talk."

"And what does talk change, Cat?" I ask with a hint of sarcasm. "What will it give me? Huh? Nothing."

"Talking about it will help you get everything out of your own head so you can process it piece by piece. You're overwhelmed by loss, and even if you don't talk to me or Gretchen, you should talk to someone—anyone." She moves closer, her eyes are begging me to hear her. "You're my best friend in the entire world. There's literally nothing I wouldn't do for you. If I could shoulder this for you, I would. You've been through so much and no one faults you for shutting down. I stood by, watching you close yourself off when we didn't know about Quinn, but he's alive, Ashton. He fought so hard to come back to you. He needs you and you need him. I'm asking you, please don't shut him out. Let him carry some of your pain, don't seclude yourself when it's unnecessary."

My heart is racing as I listen and allow myself to acknowledge that, deep in my soul, I know she's right. If I push Quinn away, I can't blame him when he finally goes. The thing is, I need to be the one who controls this. His leaving is inevitable. It'll happen whenever his guilt ebbs. I may have agreed to go to Virginia Beach, but Gretchen is there and will let me stay with her when

Quinn walks. Hopefully, I'll have a new job down there and it'll be fine.

There's no reason to come back to New York. I'm done with this city.

"I appreciate the advice, but I'm doing what I think is right."

She pushes her dark brown hair back and nods. "I see. So, you're doing the opposite of what I said?"

"Don't lecture me, Cat."

Her breath pushes from her chest. "Fine. I won't. You know, even with you being . . . well, pretty much a bitch, I will still be here to pick the pieces up. You'll have to do a lot worse than this if your goal is to be alone."

Just then, Jackson and Quinn emerge with Erin crying. Her little wails grow louder and Jackson's face shows the worry, and then I see Quinn.

His eyes are troubled, and his jaw tight as he looks down at her. I can see the sadness etched in his face. The longing gaze at the baby in his friend's arms breaks me a little further.

It's this moment when I know that, no matter what he says, he'll want this and I'll end up just the girl who couldn't give it to him.

"Ashton." Quinn says my name with a sigh as I look out the window.

I've been sitting here for over an hour, pretending to read. I can't tell you what the book is about since I've been at the same spot since I started. My mind wandered as I stared at the people on the street, each one of them living, walking, moving in a city that's brimming with life while I feel vacant. Another week has passed . . . another week of no baby. Another week of Quinn worrying constantly and me falling deeper into despair without the strength to stop it.

"Yes?" I respond.

"I asked if you were hungry."

"No," I answer and then turn back.

He moves closer, his hand brushing my hair back before settling on my neck. "Talk to me, sweetheart."

He asks me this each day, and I try, but I have zero fucks to give. "We talk."

"No we don't."

He's right, but I don't want to talk. "I'm tired."

"Because you don't sleep and you think I don't notice."

My eyes widen a bit in surprise. I didn't think he did. I go to bed with him, lie there, close my eyes, and do my best to keep my breathing even. Even when I do manage to sleep a bit, I usually wake from a dream of a child that will never be.

Why would I ever want to sleep and subject myself to that? At least when I'm awake, I can control it and force away anything that will hurt. As each day passes, it's a little easier to stay in the numbness.

"Then it's clear you're not sleeping either," I toss back.

"No, I can't because my mind is filled."

I want to ask him what's keeping him up, but I see the trap. If he gives me something then I'll be expected to give something too.

I'm good.

Since Catherine and Jackson left, it's just been us.

The two of us. Alone in this apartment as we pack.

The saddest thing for me is that we came all this way for nothing. Yesterday, when we were cleaning out the kitchen, I caught myself staring at him, wondering if he'd ever find someone else. His dark brown hair is longer and his beard has grown out. I'm sure that, in time, the fire will light back in his eyes, and he'll find happiness again.

At that thought, my heart broke a bit.

I love him. I will love him until the day I die. That much will never change, but I won't do to him what he did to me.

I won't push him to be something he's not like I tried to do before. It's what caused us to fall apart before, and now I know that I was selfish to ever ask it. I wanted a family when he wasn't ready. Now, I'm the one who isn't ready, and he can't ask the same of me.

Once again, we're back in this place, where one of us is half out the door. Only now it's so much worse because I know what us loving each other without restraint feels like.

I've felt his warmth, bathed in it, and it's something that never grows cold. Quinn won't ever be warm enough to melt the ice around my soul.

My eyes close, and I turn my head. He'll get the picture and let me be, which has been the way he's handled me all week. Like I'm a piece of broken glass that will shatter if jostled too hard.

"So, that's it?" Quinn asks with an edge to his voice.

"What's it?" I look back at him, confused by the sudden shift.

"This," he says as though I should know what he's talking about. "You're giving up. You're going to let all the love and hell we've been through just . . . go without a fight? Make it all fucking meaningless?"

"Fine. Why aren't you sleeping?" I ask.

He sinks down in front of me. "Because I can't fucking breathe, Ashton. I'm losing you. We lost the baby. I'm doing whatever I can to get you to break out of this and rage. You quit your job. I was kidnapped, for Christ's sake. All of this is weighing on me, but the thing that I can't . . . handle . . . is that you might hate me."

My lips part, and I stare at him. There, in his eyes, is a man who is falling apart. He shouldn't be sad, I have that part handled. I lift my hand to touch his face, the beard scratching my palm. "You need to shave."

Slowly, Quinn's lids fall as though he's in agony. "No, I need you, Ashton. I *need* you."

I want to tell him he has me for as long as he wants. I want to pour my heart out to him, but it's not even beating anymore. He's my whole world, and when he goes, I will be forever dead inside. All of this is on the tip of my tongue, but I swallow it.

I won't add to his guilt. That would be selfish and cruel. He doesn't need to stay with me out of obligation. I mean, what would everyone think if he walked away now? That he abandoned his girlfriend after the loss of our child, that's what.

Quinn wouldn't do that.

Not after he spent months proving he loved me.

And he did.

God did he ever. He loved me so hard I thought that maybe I wouldn't break. Those days when finding him consumed me, I wondered if maybe I would find a way to be fine once he was home. There was this small sliver of hope that his arms could heal it all. Quinn could battle away the hurt and sadness.

But it wasn't that way.

In fact, once I found him, I felt completely void.

There was nothing else to focus on other than the loss we'd endured, and I found a way to push myself into oblivion.

"I'm right here," I tell him.

"No, baby, you're not. You're a million miles away where I can't reach you."

"I want . . ."

I want it all to go away.

I want to feel his warmth.

I want none of this to be reality.

The things I desire can never be, so there's no point in telling him. The real truth is that I want to be left alone.

"What do you want?" he urges. I shake my head, refusing to open my mouth to voice any of it. "I can carry both our pain, I'm strong enough, but you have to let me," Quinn says as he brushes his thumb across my lip.

He may think that, but there's no way he could carry this load. It's far too heavy. Ten men couldn't even lift the weight that lives inside me. I may be crushed, but I don't have to do it to him too.

"And what if you crumble under the weight of my grief?"

"Then you'll have to help me back up. That's how this works. When you love someone, you shoulder what they can't and you are there to pick them up when they need it."

The first tear in over a week fills my vision. I picture this man I love, hunched over as he tries to lift me. I see it so clearly as his blue eyes watch me, begging for me to give just a piece over to him. He would struggle, but he would never give up. He'd take the broken bones and strain just to give me an inch.

I don't deserve his efforts.

Quinn moves his hand up, brushing away the bead of moisture. "Trust me not to let you down."

A small hiccup releases from my throat. I'm trying so hard to hold it back because I'm afraid of what will happen if I let even a drop of the flood free.

Some say grief washes over us like a wave, but it's more akin to a tsunami. It comes with enough force to knock down buildings. The tide rises, and you can't do anything but hold on to something on higher ground. Then the water surges to my neck, and I thought maybe that was as high as it would go. I tried treading water, kicking, keeping my head back, but when the water receded, I realized I had been swept out into the sea.

Quinn has managed to buoy me just long enough for me to take a gasp of air. He did it the day we found him. I breathed that day.

I drew the next breath when he kissed me and told me he loved me.

Right now, he has me back up, my head is fully out and there's almost this idea that the shore is much closer.

"It's not you that I don't trust," I confess. "I worry that you won't be able to handle it, and if I unload any of it, then who will pick it back up when you leave?"

He shakes his head. "I'm not leaving."

"I'm not going to get better."

"Why do you think that?"

"Because this . . . this kind of hurt? It doesn't go away. I will never be the same again. Don't you get it? I'm barely breathing."

Quinn lifts me so that I'm standing in front of him. His arms are tight around my back and then he crushes his lips to mine. He kisses me so hard that I'm forced to hold on to him so I don't fall. I try to fight off the heat that builds. I don't want to melt, but Quinn doesn't give me a chance. Between the surprise of his attack and the passion he's exuding, I don't have any resistance.

My fingers delve into his hair, holding his head to me.

His lips move down to my neck. "That's it, *fragolina*, feel me."

Then his lips are over mine again, his tongue pushing into my mouth. His fingers press into my spine, fusing me to his chest. The rapid pace of my heart tingles in my chest as though I've been shocked.

Quinn acts like a defibrillator, and the current coursing through me causes me to gasp.

"Quinn, stop," I say as I try to push away.

"No," he practically roars and then he moves me to the window, my back hits the cold glass, and his body presses flush against mine, so warm in contrast. "Don't pull away. I'll give you the breath you need. I'll warm you. I'll do whatever it takes, just let me. Let me be your heart."

He is my heart.

He's my everything.

He's the only reason I'm breathing right now, and he's also the one thing I can't let in if I have any hope of making it through this.

I re-erect the walls he tore down for that brief time and then turn my head so he can't kiss me again. "Please, stop."

Quinn takes a step back, hiding his hurt a fraction too late to keep it from me. Then he moves closer, but he doesn't touch me. "I'm sorry."

"I'm sorry, I really am." I hate myself, once again. He was doing everything right and then I realized how far he got. "I need time."

"Time to push me away more?"

"Time to . . . I don't know. It's only been a few weeks, and today . . . today would've been our ultrasound to see her. We can't see her, Quinn. She's gone, and it hurts. Okay? It hurts so much, and when I think I'll be okay again, another blow comes. I don't want to hurt you. I don't want to hurt at all, but all I feel is pain and sadness and anger."

He lifts his hand as if to touch me, but then he drops it. "I love you, and I would do anything to stop the pain."

"I love you too."

I wish that love could be enough.

chapter twelve

"NOTHING I DO SEEMS TO HELP HER," I ADMIT TO BEN AS I'm walking to the apartment after stopping at the store. "She won't talk to me. She won't let me do anything. She says she's fine and doesn't want to discuss it."

When she informed me that she quit her job? I sat there, stunned and unable to say anything. She was reasonable, at least in her rationalization as to why she couldn't perform her job anymore. I get it to some extent. Her entire life was about fertility and children. I don't know if I could handle being in a field that required me to watch something I couldn't have time and time again.

But then I think about Ben and how he didn't let his injury destroy his life. He fought through it, and I'm hoping he can give me some guidance.

"She's angry, man. I mean, can you blame her?"

"No, but she quit her job. She's not reckless. She doesn't act and think later. She loves this city but listed her apartment the day after we talked about moving. It's just . . . unlike her."

He sighs. "Maybe she knows that you'll be there to catch her as she falls."

"Of course I will."

There's no question about it. I will be here through it all because she'll come out on the other side. I know it. Sure, we can't have kids and that is a blow, but kids were always an abstract for me. It wasn't until she told me she was pregnant that I ever saw it as a reality.

Am I sad? Fuck yeah. I wanted this baby and the happiness it was bringing to Ashton. That child brought us back together in a way I didn't think could ever happen. Now, I'm afraid the loss will tear us apart.

"Then just be there for her. Let her cry or be angry or be silent. I know it's hard when the choices are taken from us. If you wanted to still be a SEAL, with everything you were, and then it was ripped away because of something out of your control, you'd be like her."

I stand outside the building, looking at the glass windows, wondering if she's staring out in a daze like she does every day. She sits in that chair and pretends to do something, but I see her—despondent.

When we kissed the other day, I thought that maybe it was a breakthrough. I felt her respond. Her body came to life, and I hoped that we were turning a corner. If there was still passion, then we needed time and patience.

But she pulled back, and since then, she's even further away from me. At night, she'll sometimes let me wrap my arm around her, but she's started pulling away a few minutes after she thinks I've fallen asleep.

I miss the girl who would literally wrap her limbs around me as though clinging to me gave her happiness.

"I don't know how to help."

"She has to help herself. I know it's a cliché and fucking infuriating, but it's true. Ashton has to accept her situation and find a way through it. This is her coping, whether you like it or not."

"I love her, Ben."

"I know, man. And there is nothing worse than watching someone you love in pain. Gretchen is my fucking world, and when she's sad, I swear that it's worse than losing my leg."

"I would give anything to take it away for her."

He goes quiet for a second, a moment of understanding seems to pass between us. "Then be patient. It's not a quality many of us have, but she needs to see you're not going anywhere. She's going to have some days where you're going to want to run, but don't."

Ashton is a professional when it comes to getting me to bend to her will. She's very good at pushing me away or shutting herself out from the world. I have no doubt that this is only the beginning. I've fought too hard and loved her too long to let her go.

"I don't think I could live without her. Even if this is the new her."

"It won't be. She'll snap out of it. Maybe the move to Virginia Beach will be good for her. I know Gretchen and Catherine are worried and they'll do whatever they can to help."

Catherine called me yesterday because Ashton won't call anyone back. She just sends a text that she's busy packing.

She's not.

She's busy wallowing.

"If you saw her, you wouldn't even recognize her."

Ben releases a deep sigh. "You know, that's sometimes how it goes. Look at how Aaron dealt with his trauma. Thank god she's not hitting you over the head, right?"

"I would prefer that to the silence."

I would do anything to get her to find that spark again.

"Be careful what you wish for. Right now, she might be in denial or some form of it, but anger will come, and that will be a whole other side of crazy. She's grieving her life, buddy. It's a tough road, but walk it with her."

I'm trying to do that.

"Thanks for listening."

"Anytime," Ben says without pause. "Quinn . . . how are you holding up?"

I go silent for a second. "I'm doing fine."

"Really? Because you lost a child too. You weren't there, and I can't imagine you're doing fine."

Leave it to Ben to call me out. Liam has been asking, but he drops it when I say I'm handling things.

The truth is I'm fucking furious. I want to rip someone's arms off and beat them with them. I'm so angry there are times I can't see straight. I loved that baby. I had plans for our lives. There's a ring sitting in a box that I was going to put on her finger. My timing and plans were perfect. We were going to go to New Jersey, have dinner with her parents, and then take a trip to the beach. I wanted to make the best memory possible for her.

Now, I can't say if she'd even smile if I proposed.

I want to marry her. I want to give her the life we talked about. Nothing about how I feel for her has changed.

"All I'm worried about right now is Ashton."

Ben clears his throat. "Well, someone needs to worry about you because all of that shit you're pretending isn't happening . . . is. She's not the only one suffering, and you won't be any good to her if you fall to shit too."

I'm the only one who isn't fucking falling apart. If I let myself feel any of the hell that's been building inside me, then what? Who the hell will pick up the pieces then? Who will hold her? Tell her that she's okay? Keep trying to convince her that we'll find a way? No one.

"What do you want me to say?" I ask.

"The truth."

"The truth is that my abduction could've done all this, at least pushed her along into it. She was alone, dealing with a little spotting, and there's this guilt that the stress of her not being able to find me sent the situation over some kind of threshold. She doesn't sleep, she barely eats, and she's so fucking sure I'm going to leave her that I don't have time to think about myself."

Ben blows out a heavy breath. "I get it. I was so worried about my ex-wife after I lost my leg that there were times I didn't even think about me. She was selfish and only worried about her and what my injury meant, so I did nothing but try to ease her. But when there was nothing else to focus on, it hit me—hard. I don't want to see that freight train run you over. There's a family here at Cole who has your back."

I'm well aware of that. Since I got back, I haven't felt as though they've abandoned me one bit. I get emails, texts, and Natalie has practically taken over the move for us. She found us a great house to rent and got all the paperwork done. She and Liam offered to let us stay with them, but there's no way Ashton or I want to be in their way. Not to mention, I saw her face when she saw Catherine's baby.

I can't imagine she'll be able to be around Aara and Shane.

"I appreciate that. I hate feeling helpless. I hate not knowing what to do and that's all I feel lately."

Ben's voice is calm and sure. "You be there and whenever she's ready to talk, listen to her. I saw a few doctors down here, but Chaplain Moore helped me a lot. She needs a neutral party to give her support. Find someone once you get here. That's my biggest piece of advice. Just don't push her too hard or you'll piss her off to the point she won't even entertain it."

"Thanks, man."

"Anytime."

If I could only get her to see that she's not fine. Hell, neither of us are, but I need to take care of her first, then I can worry about me.

I open the door to the apartment, waiting to see her sitting in that damn chair, but she's not.

I could call out for her, but I worry she might be napping. I move around the apartment, looking for her.

Slowly, I open the bedroom door, she's not there and the bathroom is empty.

I head back to the kitchen to see if she left a note, but there's nothing.

Wondering if maybe she actually went out, I grab my phone and shoot off a text.

Me: Where did you go?

A second later, the buzzing alert of a text rings from the coffee table.

She wouldn't go out without her phone, would she?

Panic starts to grip me. What if she left? What if she cracked and ran somewhere? What if Aaron came back and took *her* this time?

"Ashton!" I yell, praying she'll answer me.

I rush down the hall again, throwing open the doors to see if she's packing and I missed her.

Then I head to the other hall, my heart pounding as fear like I've never known fills me.

The door on the right is open, and I glance in.

That's when I see her.

She's sitting in the middle of the floor, her legs crossed, looking at the bassinet I assembled a few weeks ago. It was a gift from her mother and father. A family heirloom that all of her cousins, nieces and nephews, and she slept in as infants. Her mother had tears in her eyes as they brought it in. Then she put the lace cover over it and it went from being wicker to soft and inviting.

"My father reinforced the base," Ashton's detached voice says.

"Yeah?"

She nods, her red hair piled on the top of her head, back hunched over as she clutches something in her hands. "He wanted to make sure that it was safe for our baby."

The break in her voice tears me apart. I stand here, watching her, hearing the pain of loss so thick in the room that it hurts to breathe. "I'm sure it would've been strong enough."

"Unlike me."

"Don't say that." I sink to my knees beside her. "You're stronger than you know."

Her tear-stained face turns to me. For the first time, she's not wearing a façade. All of what she feels is there. The pain that radiates from her would incinerate anyone, but I fight against it because I would burn next to her if she needed me to.

I promised her I'd shoulder it, and I'll be damned if I let her down.

"We should pack it. You know, bring it back to my parents because . . . we don't need it and maybe someone else will."

"We can do that if you want."

Ashton sniffs and then looks down at her hands. "I bought this last week," she explains as she grips the tiny item. "I thought it was cute and now . . . I want . . ."

"What is it?" I ask, keeping my voice even. She's talking, and I will do anything to keep it going. The sound of her voice is like music to my ears that have felt deaf since she shut down. I want to hear it and put it on repeat so I don't forget the sound.

She lifts the little piece of fabric, and I nearly lose it. There is a baby shirt that has a skeleton frog holding a trident, the same skeleton tattoo on my back that symbolizes a SEAL. Under the picture, it says: "My daddy can kick your daddy's ass."

"I thought . . ." Ashton's voice cracks. "I thought it would be a fun first photo."

As her head turns to me, the red in her normally white eyes guts me. "I would've loved it."

She nods quickly. "I know because you would've loved that our daughter knew how great you were. But what do I do with it? Do I burn it? Throw it away? Rip it to shreds?"

I take her chin in my thumb and forefinger, keeping her eyes on mine. "We hold on to it."

"What for, huh? There's no baby that will ever wear it. We don't have a child, Quinn, and we never will."

"Still, we keep it."

She shakes her head, tears falling. "Why? So we can remember? I want to forget it all. Please, help me forget it."

My chest aches so badly I worry it'll break. I look at her, feeling so low, and I can't stop her from going deeper into despair. My hand moves across her face, wiping the moisture from her tears, and I can't hold back. My emotions are bubbling to the top, my breathing is shallow as my heart races.

"That's not the way it works, sweetheart. It won't ever be

something we forget. All we do is remember everything," I say as a tear falls down my cheek. "We hold on to how much we love that child and each other. We allow that child to live on through us. It's not easy, but I don't want to forget. We have to fight, Ashton."

Her tears fall more freely, and another burns a trail down my cheek. It's the pain of losing it all. Of having something in our grasp, the happiness we were so sure would come, only to have it end with devastation. I think of the child I dreamed of.

I imagine her red hair in pigtails and how she would've sounded as she called for her daddy. If it were a boy, he would've learned to fight and shoot. I picture us at the range as I teach him the basics.

More than anything, I hear their laughter. The sound of the child's giggles as we loved it. It was all there, right on the tips of our fingers, but we lost it.

"I can't hold on," Ashton admits.

I let all of the grief that I've been smothering rise up. "We have to because I loved that baby, Ash. I loved it and wanted it and I refuse to believe this was all for nothing."

"I'm trying."

We both are. We're trying and failing, but I can't surrender. I need her to feel the same and I worry she doesn't.

"I love you, and I don't want to lose you, but I'm watching you slip through my fingers each day," I confess, feeling weak as I try to breathe through the pain in my chest. "I can't, sweetheart. I can't lose you."

Ashton moves closer to me, her arms wrapping around my neck as she allows me to cradle her close. I hold on to her, praying she won't let go. "It hurts so much." Ashton's voice is muffled into my neck, but I can sense it all.

She's in agony. I'm supposed to protect her, and I couldn't.

I should've been there, but she was alone because I failed to go to her. "I'm so sorry," I say into her hair. "I'm so fucking sorry. I failed you, sweetheart. I wasn't there. I wasn't there, and I . . ." I trail off because I'm falling apart.

We hold each other, the hurt surrounds us as our reality is brought forward. I won't ease up as I pull her closer. I need her to breathe. All I hope is that she can feel the love I have for her and my fear of losing it. She's in pain, and I understand this, but so am I.

For the first time, I allow this part of myself to accept the truth. I'm angry, sad, and want to go back in time. I'd change everything about that day.

I never would have left that bed like she asked. I would have held her close, made sure she was never scared or stressed. If things had happened anyway, it would've been me who comforted her.

Maybe that's why we're breaking.

I wasn't there.

I didn't keep the people in my life safe, just like I didn't keep King in that Humvee safe. I survived, and for what? To let the people I love down.

I won't let that happen again. I'll protect her and heal this. I will never let her wonder if I'm going to be around.

"I'm here now, Ashton," I promise her. "I'm here, and I won't leave, don't fucking leave me. I need you."

I'm struggling to get ahold of myself. My head is buried in her hair, and I inhale the flowery scent. I cling to the familiarity of it and pray I never know what it's like not to have this.

Ashton squirms, and I lean back, afraid I'm crushing her. I can't look into her eyes and allow her to see the shame. I won't let her shoulder a scrap of guilt over that. Then there's a seed of hope that settles inside me.

She trusted me to hold her as she cried and gave me some of her pain.

Then another truth hits me, she was right about the weight of it. It's heavier than I ever imagined, but it hasn't crushed me.

I touch her face, holding her cheeks and pushing the tears away.

"I'm so afraid to feel."

"I'm so afraid that, if you don't, you'll never come back."

Ashton shakes her head, shoving my hands away, and looks back at the bassinet. Her arms wrap around her stomach as her eyes close.

I sit beside her, unsure of what else to do. How different this day is from the day the bassinet was brought here.

"I'm weak like the base was, I lost it all, and . . . I hate myself. I'm so empty, so alone, and so fucking sad." My hand reaches out to take hers. Our fingers lace, and she sobs. "I hate myself. I hate this world. I hate this bassinet and that my baby will never be in it."

"Maybe there won't ever be," I say carefully. She turns to me, wonder in her eyes. "But you're not empty and you're not alone. My heart is just as heavy, but I know that we'll make it through this. We don't have any other options."

Another tear falls down her face. "You would've been a great father."

My heart thuds, and I fight back the urge to scream. "Only because I would have been doing it with you."

She leans into my side, and I wrap my arm around her, holding her tight. I allow another tear to roll down my face in memory of the child that will never know how much we loved them and how much we mourn their loss.

chapter thirteen

ASHTON

"You move to Virginia in three days, and you haven't said a word about your job," Mom says as she spoons the chicken stew into a bowl.

What's there to say? I'm unemployed—or, as Clara says, on a leave of absence. She wouldn't accept my resignation. She explained that I needed to give her at least three months of medical leave before she'd speak of long-term options. Apparently, between the rest of my vacation and short-term disability, this was not up for discussion. So, it's been six weeks since my miscarriage, and once the rest of the time runs out, she can't say shit.

"I don't have a job."

She huffs. "Thanks to your friend, you still do. If you don't mess that up."

"Yeah, thank God for friends," I say as I shove a spoonful into my mouth.

Mom ignores the comment, but the look she gives me makes it clear she heard it. "You didn't bring Quinn tonight?"

I glance at the place setting beside me. "No, he's working."

In other words, it's his turn to check in on Aaron. As a unit, they decided to have him committed again, only this time, he's at a different facility that is between Virginia Beach and New York and has more options for PTSD treatments. They all thought it was best, and I . . . just don't care.

Whatever to it all.

It's my new motto on life. The more time that passes, the more I've learned to embrace being numb.

After I lost it a few weeks ago, I've gone back to my safe place. When I'm there, everything seems peaceful. It's nice and calm and nothing riles me. Nothing makes me angry. I don't have to fight. Quinn has been trying, bless his heart, but after I closed the door to the bassinet room, I closed my heart off again.

"At least one of you is," she says, and I eat another spoonful.

"Yes, Mom, Quinn is working and I'm taking some paid time off while I figure out what I want to do next."

She sits. "In Virginia Beach."

"Yes, in Virginia Beach."

We told my parents last week about the move. Quinn wanted to tell them sooner, but I thought it best to wait. I wasn't sure we'd still be together by moving day and I wanted to be sure we had somewhere to live. Once it became clear that both were happening, we told them. My mother cried, whereas my father seemed genuinely happy about it. He said something about moving on with life. I wasn't listening too closely. Quinn handled most of the discussion as I pretended to eat.

However, he's not here tonight, which means I have to manage to at least appear engaged.

"Did you see Clara for your checkup this week?"

"Yes, she said I've healed nicely."

My body has at least. Six weeks is all it takes apparently. That's all my insides needed to heal. If only my heart could feel that way. In that time, I've only grown colder, sadder, and less . . . alive.

"That's good. I'm glad there weren't any complications."

I nod once. "Yup. Good thing."

My mother's smile falls. I can tell she's trying to keep her thoughts to herself. "Are you happy about the move?"

I shrug. Happy? No. I don't even know what happy looks like anymore. She wouldn't believe me if I lied, so it's best if I appear blasé about it. "It is what it is."

"And what exactly are you right now?"

I look up, watching her watch me. "What does that mean?"

"Exactly what I said, darling. You're allowing your loss to consume you. You're basically nothing, so I'm asking what you think you are. Are you the girl who would defiantly tell me no and walk out? Are you the girl who would fight to the death if someone she loved was in trouble? Surely, you're not this void of a person in front of me, right?"

"Can we not do this?" I ask. I am really not in the mood. My mother might be the only person alive who could break through to me, which was why I tried to cancel this week. I knew if she got me alone she'd find an opportunity. It's why she sent my father to his hunting cabin. He never goes during the week.

Ever.

This was all a ploy. Now, I'm starting to wonder if Quinn's check-in on Aaron wasn't arranged as well.

"When would you prefer to do it? Next week? Tomorrow? Never?"

"Never works."

Mom doesn't react. She places her spoon down, grabs a piece of bread, and butters it before putting it in front of me. It's a simple task. One that wouldn't mean anything to a normal person, but this is us. My mother doesn't do anything without purpose. She knows that bread with butter is my comfort. I haven't had a single slice since that day.

I don't want comfort.

I don't want bread and butter that I dip in . . . soup.

I look down at the bowl, another twinge of awareness dawns on me. "Soup, bread with butter, I'm surprised you went for stew instead of pasta fagioli."

"I thought that might be too obvious." Her eyes never move from mine. "It's been weeks, and you have pulled yourself so far into this place of protection that I felt drastic measures were in order."

"You won't get me out, Ma."

She smiles as though she has zero doubts she will. "Eat your bread."

I cross my arms in defiance and anger. "I don't want bread."

"Take a bite, and I'll talk. If you stop eating even once, I'll wait you out and we'll be here for days."

This is her plan, to make the stubborn side of me rise in defiance. To make me so angry that I do as she says, break down, and become the Ashton I once was. She of all people should know that won't happen.

I take the bread, raise to my mouth, and bite down. I wait for the feelings to come because she knows my weakness, but they don't.

I feel . . . nothing.

Relief floods me. I'm immune to bread, and I couldn't be happier about it.

I chew another piece, grinning at her with a look of glee that she tried to play me and it didn't work.

"As I was saying, I don't think you could fight if you wanted to because you've given up. I never thought you were a quitter."

Something inside me twists with indignation. I'm not a quitter. I'm doing what I can to survive. I didn't jump off a building or end my life because I was hurting. No, I found a way to cope. Is it the best? Probably not. Am I going to lose everything else? Most likely. Do I care? Maybe.

I place the food down and clasp my hands in front of me. "I'm enduring. I'm not perfect nor do I pretend to be. I don't know how to be happy right now. I can't find the strength to do anything more than this. I get up, shower, eat, and breathe."

My mother comes around the table, her eyes are warm and there's so much worry in them. "I almost lost you, Ashton. Imagine the pain you're in but one hundred thousand times worse. Imagine if you loved that child, held her, raised her, and then she was gone. Can you grasp that I, too, am struggling? Not only because I thought you might die but also because I knew you living would cause you pain. God forgive me, but I prayed you'd live because I couldn't endure losing you."

A tear falls down her face. "Mom," I whisper.

"I want you to understand that we're all grieving with you. I know it's nothing like you're feeling, but I know what it's like to lose a child. I also know what it's like to be defeated."

The twist is now becoming tighter in my gut. My mother doesn't need to cry. She's done everything for me. "I want to feel better," I confess.

I don't exactly like being this way. I just don't know any other way. I'm too scared to step forward.

"It's a choice. You can wallow in grief or you can fight through it. There's nothing easy about any of it, but what you're doing now will only hurt you in the long run."

"When does it get easier?" I ask, praying she can give me an answer.

My mother's hand touches my cheek. "When you start to feel it and deal with it. Until then, you'll stay in this purgatory. Now, eat."

And then I do, thinking about what she said. Can I live through it? That's the thing I can't answer.

"What do you think?" Natalie asks as we walk around the house she picked. "I thought it was a good reflection of your style."

It's a fully renovated home right on the bay. The owner was smart to take advantage of the view when they decided on floor-to-ceiling windows that overlook the water.

"It's really beautiful," I tell her as I take it all in.

"You're only about ten houses down from Liam and me, too. I thought it would be nice . . . if you want . . . to be able to have people close. Plus, Gretchen and Ben are looking in this area now too, so we'd all be together."

Natalie is sweet, and I appreciate that she's being so kind about all of this. "It's great."

I move into the kitchen, which reminds me a bit of the apartment in New York. It has clean lines and white cabinets and countertops. The floors are a gray slate look, and it has exposed ducts.

Quinn comes behind me, wrapping his arms around my shoulders. His voice is low as he whispers. "If you don't like it, she won't be upset."

I shake my head and attempt to smile as I look up from behind me. "I really like it."

"Good." He grins down at me.

Since the dinner with my mother, I've been trying to feel little bits of emotion at a time. I'm still not sleeping and food really doesn't appeal to me, but around Quinn, I'm trying to appear more . . . human.

The ride down here, I held his hand and used every ounce

of strength I had to hold a conversation. He asked about what I wanted to do with my time once we were moved in, and I tried to come up with something. We discussed his work schedule, and I could see a sliver of relief on his face.

Trying to keep that going for seven hours has drained me.

Natalie releases a heavy sigh. "Well, I have to get the kids from the sitter, but I'm happy you like the place. I know you don't get your stuff for a few days, so if you need anything, please let me know."

He releases me and pulls her in for a hug. "Thanks, Lee, but there's no need," Quinn says quickly. "Ashton and I are heading out."

"We are?" I ask.

My heart starts to race a little because he didn't say anything. He just said we were going here. I can't do any more acting. I want to sit in the dark for a bit and collect myself.

"Yes."

"Oh, you didn't . . ." I force myself to swallow, "say anything, so I didn't know."

"On that note, I'll be going. Don't hesitate to call me." Natalie looks at me pointedly. "I know people always say that to be polite, but this isn't that time. I'm right down the beach and I plan to come by unannounced because that's who I am. Okay?"

God, I'm going to need to be medicated. "I don't have a choice, do I?"

Her lips tip up into a smile. "Not really."

With that, Natalie heads out the door, giving us a wave before closing it. I turn back to Quinn. "Where are we going?"

He moves toward me, his eyes watching my expression closely. "I think the two of us have been through enough hell the last few weeks and need a break, don't you?"

How I wish it were that simple. There's no break we can

take that'll make me forget how, if I touched my stomach, there would no longer be a child growing.

Still, I need to try to at least do what I can to make everyone believe I'm fine so they can let me be.

"I guess."

"Not the answer I was hoping for, but I'll take it." He smiles and then grabs the bag I had placed down when we got here. "Let's go."

Please, God, let it be somewhere I can hide in the crowds.

chapter fourteen

QUINN

W E'RE ABOUT TWENTY MINUTES FROM OUR DESTINATION when Ashton begins to fidget with her hands. I'm not so sure this was a good idea, but it's the only one I have. We have a week with no furniture, and I told Mark we needed some time away.

It was Natalie who suggested I take Ashton to the house my grandmother still owns in the Outer Banks of North Carolina, which I hope ends up being a stroke of brilliance. It was a magical place for her and Liam, and I'm hoping the quiet beaches of Corolla will be the same for us.

"Where are we going?"

"My family has a beach house in Corolla, I thought it might be a great place for us to escape."

She tightens her fingers until the knuckles turn white. "It should be great. Just the two of us."

I clench my jaw because I'm trying so fucking hard. I've given her space, pushed her, talked to her, waited her out, and we go nowhere. After the night in the spare bedroom, I hoped we had turned a corner, but it's starting to look like I'd been wrong.

She's not mean or even cold. She snuggles into me each night and is willing to hold my hand, but it's not her.

Ashton was fire.

This is ice.

We pull into the parking spot for the house, and she does her version of a smile. As if I don't see that it's fake. I've let her think she's fooling me, but I'm not buying it.

This has to stop here.

I have to get her to finally break or we're going to be what does.

I grab the bags, and she trails behind me. The two-story beach house that sits on stilts is everything I remember. My grandpa bought it for Nana and made everyone promise to always treat it like a jewel. So, we do. Each year, my cousins or I come and do something to keep it maintained. Last year, I repainted the outside the same blue it's been for eighty years.

"What do you think?" I ask Ashton as we enter.

"It's gorgeous."

And it's the first time I believe anything that's come out of her mouth in a while.

"I did all the tile work." My voice beams with pride.

She moves into the kitchen, running her hand over the black granite. We did white cabinets to match the doors that open onto the deck out front. My cousin had the idea to blow out the front door and make it basically a wall of windows to overlook the ocean, and by the way her eyes are staring out, I can tell it was a good one.

"Quinn, this is amazing. The view is stunning."

I nod. "Wait until you see it from the bedroom upstairs."

Her eyes study mine before she turns them back out at the sea. I can't resist the urge to hold her. I move toward her and stand so her back is to my front.

All she has to do is lean back, fall a little, and she'll see that I'll catch her.

I wait, trying to be as patient as I can.

I feel the tension rolling off her, and instead of doing what I silently beg, she turns. Her blue eyes are soft as her hands lift tentatively and then rest on my chest.

My heart is beating so hard as I let her lead this. The last time I kissed her, I was the one pushing, this time, I'm stepping back, but it doesn't mean all the way.

"Tell me what you need, and it's yours," I offer her the opening.

I watch her retreat back into her head. Before she can answer, her phone rings.

"It's Clara," she says.

I walk outside, giving her some privacy, and stare at the sea. I loved coming here as a kid. It was a place where everything made sense. There were no rules other than come check in when the lifeguards left. All of it was so easy. Nothing like it is today for me.

There is no joy, though. In place of it, there's a pit in the bottom of my stomach. I want to push it back, but I've been trained to rely on my senses. Sometimes, I think she's afraid of me. That she's convinced herself of something and won't see any other options.

Ashton talks about me leaving or realizing how damaged she is.

Does she truly believe that we're not all broken? All we can do is hold the pieces together as tight as we can and pray the cracks don't grow.

After about fifteen minutes, Ashton comes out. "You okay?"

"I'm . . . not sure."

Worry starts to seep through. Did she take some test before

we left and didn't tell me? Maybe there was something with the job she didn't mention? With everything that has happened over the last few months, it could be anything.

I'm not worried about finances. After growing up with relatively no money, I refused to be careless with money and have saved everything. While other team guys were buying trucks and shit with their bonuses, I was banking it.

There have only been two big purchases I've made: my truck and the engagement ring for Ashton. Otherwise, it's been accumulating and invested. So, if she lost her job, we're just fine.

"What did she say?"

Ashton sighs and looks away. "They need help."

"Who needs help?"

Her eyes meet mine. "A clinic in Virginia Beach. Their embryologist quit, and they've been unable to find anyone to run the lab. Apparently, Clara said it's a dire situation because they're losing viable eggs."

I'm not sure what to say or really what any of it means, but it sounds like this is a chance for her to do something again. I know she doesn't want to work in IVF anymore, and to some extent, I get it, but I want her to have something that fulfills her.

"Did you give her an answer?"

"I'm not doing it."

"I didn't think you would." I decide to push back on her a little. The only time she is real is when she's angry.

"What the fuck does that mean?"

"Just what I said. I didn't think you'd do it. I know you're done helping other people have kids."

Ashton's lips part as she rears back. "No, I didn't say that. I don't want to make babies anymore. It's not about helping people."

I put my hands up as though I wasn't trying to provoke her.

"Hey, no need to explain it to me. I wouldn't want you to do anything that might hurt you."

She turns around, arms crossed over her chest. "You think I should do it, don't you?"

"I think you should do *something*."

"And, yet, a week ago, you were fine with me taking some time off."

"No, you were fine with not working and said that you wanted no part in IVF."

"Clearly, Clara didn't get the memo."

I get to my feet and head toward her. "Or Clara sees that there is a need for someone who is as smart and as dedicated as you. Someone who feels it is part of who they are to help other people have something they want as badly as you did. Losing our baby was horrible and unfair, but the people who you help are grateful for what you give them."

"A lot of good it does me, right?"

I wish I could reach inside her and pull out the pain, but it's not possible. I can't do anything but sway with her and catch her when she tilts too far. "You act as though you've lost everything."

"I have!"

"You haven't lost me, your family, your friends . . . all of that is still right here, but you keep pushing us away."

"Maybe it's because I want you to leave."

"Well, too fucking bad, Ash. I'm not going anywhere."

She bites down on her lip, eyes filled with sadness. "No, I guess you're not."

"What does that mean?" My pulse spikes and I know she's saying something beneath it.

I take two steps but she retreats. "It means I'm tired and need to lie down. Thank you for this talk."

And my fucking heart breaks.

Ashton is sound asleep, and I'm . . . pissed.

I'm angry at everything and have been trying so hard to be understanding, but I'm failing. There are only two things that can remotely get me out of this, and the first isn't going to happen when she can barely look at me.

So running it is.

I tie my shoes, throw my headphones on, and go. I haven't exercised hard since my kidnapping. I've wanted to, but I was afraid to leave her for too long. I've been afraid of everything with her.

My legs push on, feet moving the sand as though I'm commanding it to make way. Rage courses through my veins as I go past families enjoying the sun, a woman lying on her towel, a guy walking leisurely with his dog—all of them seeming to look content.

There's nothing in my body that says anything close to the same. I'm furious. I've failed the same woman time and time again.

Ashton is a comet racing across the sky. I can see her—she's bright, beautiful, and wonderous, but she can't be caught. She leaves a trail behind her, reminding me that I can keep trying to chase her, but I'll never be fast enough.

God, how I thought I could be.

I was so close, I had my hand there and then the universe gave her more force to pull away.

Somehow, I find myself back in front of the house, sweat dripping down my face. I tear my shirt off, wipe my face with it, and look up, wondering if she's still asleep.

I don't know where we go from here, but I know I have to do something drastic or there won't be any way to ever get near her heart again. She's closed herself off to everything she loves—including me.

Then I see a movement in the curtains. In the wall of windows that opens all the way up, I see her silhouette. Her deep red hair is bright against the white and I can't fucking breathe.

I need her. I need her in a way I've never known. As though the last part of me has snapped and we will either recover or we'll be over. I have to get to her.

Something inside me refuses to stop, even knowing this could be the end. I push myself inside and take the stairs three at a time. The door flies open, and she turns, her lips parted and there's a bead of moisture below her eye.

"You were crying."

Ashton nods. "I guess I was."

I move closer, unwilling to give her any more space. "Do you still love me, *fragolina*?"

This isn't what I should be asking, but God, if I don't feel like her answer will be the precipice of my life.

"Of course I do."

"Do you want me to let you go?"

This answer is even more important. She might love me, and I know I love her, but I can't make things harder for her anymore. I thought waiting her out was the key. I believed that if I gave her time, she'd come around.

I've been reaching, fighting, and chasing her, but what if I'm holding her back? Losing her will fucking kill me, but destroying her would be a fate worse than death.

I love her unselfishly, which means I will do what she needs.

Ashton watches me, I can feel the tension filling the room, and then, when I think my heart can't take another second, a tear rolls down her face, and I know my answer.

chapter fifteen

ASHTON

I'M LOSING HIM AGAIN. I CAN SEE THAT I'M BREAKING HIM, AND it's shredding what is left of my heart.

But now that it's happening and I'm face to face with it, a new wave of sadness crashes over me.

I don't *want* to let him go. Another thing taken from me will hurt, regardless of the shell I've created around myself, I was stupid to think when this day came it wouldn't cause me to ache.

I watched him run with a force I haven't seen in far too long. It was as though his body was fueled by something far deeper than the urge to exercise. Even from my window, I could see his jaw, tight and filled with anger.

I'm not fool enough to think it has nothing to do with me.

I wept for the man I love. Tears fell down my cheeks as I saw the damage I'm doing to him. With each pump of his legs, I felt the distance growing between us.

Now, I have to do whatever I can to close the gap.

"Is that what you want?" I ask with a shake in my voice.

"I asked you if you want me to let you go."

He's trying to give me power. I've had so many decisions taken from me, and I wish someone would take this one away from me as well.

My chest heaves as I look at him. This man who has battled so many things, given me more than I ever hoped for, and I'm choking on my thoughts.

The truth is, I never want him to leave. I want to stay in his arms every single day because I love him. He is everything I want and need, but I am no longer the girl who deserves him.

Quinn's love is a gift, and I've neglected it.

"I don't want to lose you." I take a step closer, my eyes leaking a steady stream of tears because I know that I have to let him go before I ruin him.

As selfish as needing him makes me, I can't stop myself. I want one more time with Quinn, to be alive in his arms, to touch him and bask in his love. I'm a horrible person, but I push all of that aside.

My hand lifts to his face, and I touch the stubble, reveling in the coarseness of the hair. He's so beautiful.

"Ashton." He says my name with reverence. A prayer from his lips that I haven't earned.

"Shh." My finger covers his lip. "No more questions. No more wonder. Make me feel you, Quinn. Make me forget everything but you."

He doesn't hesitate. A second later, he has me in his arms, and his lips are on mine. I kiss him, giving as much as taking, letting him fill me to the brim with everything. I feel his hesitancy, emotions, love, and determination.

It swirls between us as his hands press against my back, keeping me tight against him.

The sound of hunger erupts from his throat as his tongue slides into my mouth. I drink in his taste. His breathing is labored, and I don't know if it was from the run, our talk, or the fact that we're both surrendering to each other.

All of the past weeks slip away as his lips graze against my skin. Gone is the loss, grief, and sadness. It's all replaced with him.

"I fucking love you, Ashton."

"I love you."

That's the only thing that's been constant. I love him. I just don't love myself.

His hands slide into my hair, and as his fingers wrap around the strands, he tilts my head to the side. I revel in the way his tongue pushes against mine. We both battle each other before he breaks away, sliding down the column of my neck.

Quinn's teeth nip against my smooth skin, biting softly as he gets to the base. His tongue leaves a trail as he goes to my shoulder, moving the straps of my tank top down. "God, I've missed you." I close my eyes, fingers in his dark hair. "I've missed your taste, your smell, the feel of your skin against mine."

I shiver and kick against the current that is threatening to take me away from him. This time, I don't want to let it pull me out to the safe, calm waters where I drift. This might be our last time, so I need to remember, absorb, and savor it all.

"Kiss me," I beg.

He does. He kisses me like he's a starved man and I'm his last meal. It's been so long, and he's been patient with me, never once pushing me into something I couldn't handle. He's settled for chaste kisses and snuggling.

When his lips leave mine, he's panting. "Do you want me to stop?"

Quinn has always been ravenous when it came to us sexually, and right now, I want to unleash the beast.

"No. No, don't stop. Please, I'm not made of glass, and if I am, then I want you to break me."

He lifts me so my legs can wrap around his waist. Our lips

stay fused as he walks us to the bed. I grip his damp, hot skin as he lowers me.

Quinn stands, looking over me. His chest rises and falls with the effort it's taking for him to control himself.

I've been weak the last few months. The loss of the baby has beaten me down and left me in a constant state of despair, but I push that all away.

He won't give me what I need if he sees that same woman. I dig as deep as I can to bolster myself. There's no way he'll break me willingly.

"I want you so much, but fuck, Ash, you . . ."

"Need this," I say for him.

I watch the storms roll through his eyes, and I won't let him stop. I lean up, wrapping my hand behind his head, and bring our lips together. Slowly, he melts into the kiss. I coax him to stop thinking, praying he'll let his restraints slip further.

Then his warm hand moves down my front to the hem of my shirt, and I stare into his eyes as he removes it. Not wanting him to back out, I unhook my bra and fling it to the floor.

Quinn drinks me in as my breasts are bared to him.

"You're gorgeous."

I don't allow the self-doubt to seep into this moment. It doesn't matter that I have a scar on my stomach or that I'll forever feel like less of a woman. He doesn't see that, and I need it to stay that way.

My fingers move to his chest. "You're so hot." I trace the planes of his abs, loving the ridges and peaks. There's a faint scar on his side, and I press my lips to it. "I've always loved your body."

He tilts my head back. "I love you."

I know he does, which is the best and worst part of it. Somewhere, deep in his blue eyes, I see the fear lingering. I wonder if he knows what this is and will stop it.

My hands slide down to his running shorts and pull them

down. His dick springs free, and I wrap my hand around it. "Love me then."

He moves so quickly I don't have time to think. His hands tuck under my thighs, and he slides me toward the center of the bed. He pulls my shorts off, leaving us both naked.

"This isn't how I wanted this to go."

"I don't want flowers and candles," I say, brushing my finger through his hair. "I want us, and we're not that. We're anger, heat, and passion."

"Fucking hell yes we are. I'm not going to be able to hold back. Tell me now that you want this."

"I want you. All of you."

"Stay with me, Ashton."

His mouth is on mine, sealing my lips to his. Whether he means for this moment or longer, I'm not sure, but I'm grateful he didn't require a response.

Quinn's rough fingers move lower. He kneads my breast, thumbing the nipple and then pulling at it. I moan into his mouth, loving how rough he's being.

Then he slides down, his lips never leaving my skin as he swirls his tongue around my nipple. I close my eyes, letting my body absorb it all. He sucks, flicks, and grazes the sensitive flesh with his teeth. It's heaven and hell all at once—it's us.

"God, this feels so good."

He chuckles against my skin and starts to move lower. He kisses my belly, staying there, pressing another kiss to my scar and making me want to cry.

Our eyes meet, and I pray he doesn't say anything. I won't be able to hold back the tears. He has no idea the shame I see in the mirror each day. He doesn't understand that scar represents so much for me. Then his lips graze it again, and I wonder if he does understand more than I think.

The way he's loving me, all of me, including the scars is a message I hear in my heart.

I'm tense and everything inside me is yelling at me to stop this, but then he slides lower, lifting my knees and pressing his tongue to my clit. It's been so long, and the fact that I'm allowing myself to feel anything makes it so much more intense.

He moans and licks as though he's starved. Maybe we both are and need this more than either of us realize.

"Quinn," I pant, calling his name as his mouth devours me.

I feel his finger slide into me, and I tighten around him. Quinn doesn't slow his pace, he isn't gentle or sweet—he's ravenous. There's not a chance I could hold myself back, he won't let me. I start to reach the top of the mountain, seeing the peak right in my view. He pushes me, forcing me up, and when I'm there, Quinn doesn't allow me a second to stop, I go right over the edge.

I fall, feeling the most intense pleasure as I writhe beneath him. My voice is incoherent as I call his name and God only knows what else.

The ground seems so far away, and I'm weightless, but before I have time to fear the fall, Quinn is right there to catch me.

"I love you, Ashton. I love you, and I fucking need you."

I open my eyes, tears forming because of the enormity of what is happening. "I need you too."

I need this with him.

"You have to tell me this is okay."

I nod. "This is what I want."

"What is?"

"You."

He kisses me deeply, conveying with his mouth all that is in his heart. Then Quinn lines himself up at my center. I feel his hesitancy and rail against it. This might be the last time we ever have each other and there can be no holding back.

I take his face in my hands and stare deeply in his eyes. "Give me everything, Quinn."

And then he does, and it's beautiful and heart-wrenching at the same time.

chapter sixteen

QUINN

 HE SECOND I ENTER HER, EVERYTHING SHIFTS. SHE COMES alive, and I know it deep in my soul that nothing can break us now. I can sense every part of her is mine again. It's something that I've seen played out in movies but never thought was real.

It is.

It's very real, and it's happening, she's here with me. I've broken through that wall she built around herself.

This is my Ashton.

The woman who I've loved has finally returned. I hover above her, her heat surrounding me, burning me, branding me, and I'm giving it right back.

I push deeper, filling her and praying that it'll make her feel less empty. My head is pressed into her neck, breathing her scent as she kisses my skin.

"You feel so good," I tell her.

I want her to know that nothing has changed for me. I loved her then, and I'll love her forever. There's nothing that she can say or do to push me away. I want to marry her and build a life together.

She pants, and I start to lose my restraint. Being inside her is like a heaven I thought I'd never know again.

"Take me," Ashton yells. "Take me and don't let me go!"

"Never!"

I wanted the first time after our loss to be sweet so that I could show her how much I love her, but this is how we were meant to be. We aren't docile—we're fucking eruptive. Each time I thrust into her, I claim another part of her, taking what's mine—her.

There is no holding back, I can't stop the suddenness of my orgasm. It tears through me, ripping me to shreds, and I don't fucking care.

She's mine.

Always.

I savor the bite of her nails in my back as she holds on, yelling my name as she loses herself.

My heart is pounding, strength is depleted, but I lean up so I can look at her. "Are you okay?"

She nods, but there's a hesitancy in her eyes.

No. I won't do this again.

We can't go back in time, and I can't watch her retreat into the shell of a woman she was this morning. "Ashton, please don't."

"Don't what?"

"Don't go backward." I push back her hair, staring into the blue eyes that have a bit of life in them.

"I'm not . . . I'm . . . recovering."

That's just it, she's not. She's wallowing and pulling away from everyone and everything she loves. Her job, me, her friends, her family have become peripheral things when we used to be front and center.

I thought that this was her returning to me. It's been

weeks, and now that I've tasted her life again, I can't watch it slip away.

"Recover with me. You don't have to do this on your own."

"I wish it were that simple. Please let me up."

The hope and elation I felt is gone. She's doing it, and I won't be able to stop her. I move off her, and she heads into the bathroom. Minutes pass, and the longer she takes, the more I start to worry.

Maybe I hurt her.

Maybe there's something wrong.

I get to my feet and pull my shorts on, ready to go after her, but before I can get there, the door opens. What I see, breaks my heart in a way I never knew existed.

Gone is the girl who let herself go, enjoyed what we are, and felt it all. The woman who can barely force a smile without looking like she's on the edge of tears is back.

I can't fucking do it again. There's no way I can handle this.

My chest is tight, and I swear I'm going to lose my fucking mind.

"Ashton."

She puts her hand up. "Don't. I know you hate this. I know it's driving you crazy, and I see you struggling, which makes it that much harder for me. I'm watching you . . . feel this . . . and it's my fault. I know it is. I know that you're dying each day, but I'm already dead, Quinn."

I move, gripping her arms gently, but firmly enough to make her know I'm serious. "If you were dead, you would've never felt what we just did. I know you were with me the entire time."

"It doesn't matter. I'm not with you now!"

"The hell you're not. You're always with me. I fucking love you so much it's killing me. All I want is to make you happy, but

I can't do that when you refuse to even give me a chance. I'm strong enough to take it. I'm here, willing and ready, but you're so closed off to even trying. What are you gaining with this? What the hell is the point, Ashton? What can I do to show you that I'm right here and I'm not going anywhere?"

"Can you give me a baby?" she yells, her eyes are filled with the pain she tries to hide. "Can you make all of this a bad dream? Are you strong enough to turn back time and fix this? No! You can't! So, stop acting as though this is something you can fix. You can't fix me!"

I shake my head as my heart pounds in anger and frustration. "I don't want to fix you, I want to love you."

A tear falls down her cheek. "You can't love someone who doesn't exist anymore."

I refuse to believe this is what she wants. "You think you don't exist?"

"The girl I was is dead."

"Maybe so." I shrug while shaking my head. "Maybe the guy I was is gone too. Maybe none of us will ever be the same. I know what it's like to live without you, Ashton. I won't do it again. Not after what we shared. If you were really gone, the girl who was so alive in my arms . . . she wouldn't have existed." My hands cup her cheeks, rubbing away the tears with my thumbs. "You're there, *fragolina*. Underneath all that pain you've allowed to weigh you down is the woman I love. You think she's gone, but I felt her a few minutes ago."

Ashton closes her eyes and then steps out of my grasp. "This was a mistake. I should've . . . you don't deserve this."

Not again. She's going to stand here and deal with this once and for all. "You don't get to decide that for me. I choose you. I'm here because I fucking love you! We aren't a mistake, what we did just now, wasn't a mistake. Don't ever say that to me again."

"I knew this would happen," she says as she swipes another tear. "I didn't think it would be hard, but now that I've felt you again, I'm just—I'm—"

I step back into her space because I dread the next words. I see the turmoil in her posture and feel the pain in her words. "If you're thinking of leaving me, think again."

"We have to stop this. I can't pretend that this is going to work and I'm going to snap out of it. Neither can you."

I don't accept this. "We didn't come this far for this, Ashton!"

"I'm tired of trying. I want to move on."

"No you don't," I say. "You don't want to feel or go forward, you want to stay where you are."

Fire flashes in her eyes. "So what if that's true?"

"That's not life! You're the one who told me that! You're the one who gave me this hope that I could be more, now I am, and you want to walk away. We lost a baby, Ashton. We lost her and that will never change for us. You can't have a baby, I know this, but fucking hell, you have me! I'm trying so hard, and you're giving up."

She shakes her head. "I gave up weeks ago."

This isn't going to be the end. I don't care what she says. I have to snap her out of it. I'll fuck her every hour if that is what it will take to bring back that light. My body is vibrating with the need to fix this. I step toward her, gathering her in my arms, and I bring my lips down. I kiss her, pushing the determination into her, begging her with my lips to feel again.

Her hands don't clutch me this time, instead, they push away.

My chest is tight, and I struggle to breathe. Fear grips at my heart, strangling it until I'm not sure it's beating. I'm losing her. She's already halfway out the door, and if I don't do something drastic, the other half will go with it.

I rush over to my bag and pull out the black box with the diamond I bought months ago. This, again, wasn't my plan, but if she sees that I've been planning for long term, maybe she'll stop this fucking bullshit. I love her. She'll be my wife, and I'll give her everything. There's nothing in this world I won't fight through to make her happy.

She just has to stay with me. I'll find a way and make this work.

"Ashton Caputo." I drop to my knee, lifting the top of the box. "I bought this ring the day I got in a car to come to you after the IED accident. I knew then that there was no one in this world I wanted other than you. I needed to prove myself worthy of you. You say I don't deserve this, and that's a lie because it's you who deserves better than me. But here we are, still hanging on, and I'm telling you that I love you and I need you. I want to spend my entire life right beside you, no matter what that looks like." Her tears keep falling, and I stand, moving toward her. "I'm not going to ask you to marry me," I say as I pull the ring out. "I'm not going to give you the choice because there's nothing I won't do to make us work. I'll be the fight when you have none. I'll be the strength when you think there's nothing left. I'll love you enough when you can't love yourself. I'm going to marry you, Ashton Caputo, because we're infinite."

I place the ring on her finger, waiting for her to say something, but she doesn't. Ashton leans forward, her forehead pressed tight against my chest as my arms wrap around her, and I pray that she came back in the door.

chapter seventeen

ASHTON

I STARE DOWN AT MY RING, WONDERING HOW I WENT FROM one extreme to another. I swear I have whiplash from the entire thing. I'm engaged, and yet, I have no intention of staying with him.

He walks around the side of the bed, pulling the blankets down. "Come lie with me," he requests.

I do as he asks because my mind can only concentrate on one thing at a time. When I sit on the edge of the bed, I go to take my jewelry off like I always do, and he grabs my hand.

"What?"

"Don't take it off."

My stomach drops. Does he know? Can he see the wheels in my head going? Did I show my hand somehow? "Why can't I take it off?"

Quinn rubs his thumb along it. "Because I've waited a really long time to find a girl I wanted to marry. I want to know it's where it belongs."

He's killing me. He's fucking wrecking me in every way. It hurts to breathe, and I wish that the ground would open up and swallow me. All I can muster to get out is one word. "Okay."

He leans in, kissing me. "Do you like the ring?"

"I love it." And I do. I loved it the first time I saw it. He found something that was truly perfect for me.

Too bad I'm not the perfect girl to wear it.

"Good." Quinn settles next to me and pulls me into his arms. My ear presses against his chest, listening to the steady sound of his heartbeat.

I lie here, inhaling his woodsy cologne that has a small hint of cloves. I close my eyes, breathing it in and committing it to memory.

"I love you, Quinn."

He kisses the top of my head. "I love you. I'm always going to be here for you, *fragolina*. You have no idea how happy you make me, and I promise to do the same for you. Go to sleep. We are both exhausted."

"Yeah, we are."

He settles even more, gently rubbing my back, giving me comfort I don't deserve.

"Sleep, sweetheart. I've got you."

My lips won't move even though my mind is screaming at him to stop. I might have asked him to break me, but I didn't know quite what that would be like.

Now, I'm going to do the same to him, and I hate myself more than I could ever explain.

I do my best to fake sleep by evening out my breaths. The sky turns darker, the stars shine bright, and the moon is incredible.

It casts light across the ocean like a beacon to whatever will walk its way. I think about how that strip of white leads to somewhere far away and how, if I could go there, I would. I would run to a place where there weren't any problems or past hurts, a world where things would be different.

More time passes, but the sky remains the same. Quinn has

shifted, his hands are tucked under his face as he shifts to his side, and I know he's truly asleep. I look at the lines, which were so tight a few hours ago, as they relax. When he awakens, he'll never forgive me.

I wanted to argue with him before, tell him how he can't really want all that he said, but I know him. He wouldn't have let it go. He's so hellbent on making this work that he doesn't see the truth. Our hearts can never heal, and eventually, Quinn will be like I am—obliterated.

I love him too much to let that happen.

If I go now, he can find a way through it. I know that there will be a part of him that will fight against it, it's who he is. My warrior.

The man who will slay dragons, cut anyone down, and live through hell for me. The thing is, he can't see the dragon because it lives inside me and he won't allow himself to kill it. So, I have to.

I didn't know it would quite possibly kill me to do it.

It doesn't evade me that he has literally given me everything I have ever asked for. He's stood by my side, loved me, put a ring on my finger, and offered me his entire heart with no restraints. I wish I knew why I can't be happy with that, but I'm not.

Maybe it's because his happiness will end up being the final cost.

I brush my hand against his cheek, feeling his skin for what will be the last time.

The words fall from lips so faintly that I hope he doesn't stir. "It isn't because I don't love you, it's because I love you too much to hurt you any longer. I know you won't ever forgive me, but I hope that, one day, you'll understand."

Slowly and making as little movement as possible, I get out of the bed and make my way to the door. I shouldn't look back,

I should keep going, but I need to see him just once more. My heart feels as though it's being torn from my chest when I see him there. He's so peaceful and content. I would give anything to be that way.

As much as I want to stay, I can't because we will never move forward. Each time I look at Quinn, I see the life we dreamed of that we can never have. The child we wanted, the life we planned, the hearts that are now broken and can't be repaired, that's what keeps haunting me. If I go now, maybe I can create a new future where I won't be reminded at every turn of all we've lost.

"Goodbye, Quinn," I whisper to the wind.

My feet move down the stairs, but my heart remains there. I don't need it because it'll never be anyone else's but his.

Memories assault me with each step I take. The first time he kissed me. The way we looked at each other the night we met and how I couldn't keep my eyes from him. I remember the first time we slept together and the butterflies that rooted in my stomach.

Now they can fly.

Quinn has always been the man I knew I'd never get over. He imprinted himself onto my soul, and I'm not strong enough to erase him. No one would understand why I'm doing this, but there's no way I can go through the rest of my life being unfair to him. I have to make a clean break.

I get to the door where my bag sits, and I remove the ring from my finger. Only then do I allow myself to cry. The first time I saw this ring, it was a symbol of so much hope and happiness. The second time, it was nothing but a desperate Hail Mary.

My, how the times have changed.

I bring the diamond to my lips, kissing it and hoping he won't come after me so that this can be our goodbye.

I place it down, lingering for a moment because, in another life, I wouldn't be getting in a cab to leave. I'd be in bed with him, loving him, kissing him, giving him everything because he is the best man I know. This isn't that life, and I don't want to be the target of his resentment.

So, I must go.

I gather my bags and walk out of the door. My tears fall faster as I make my way to the cab.

"Where to?" The driver turns to look at me.

"Anywhere but here."

He starts to move but stops when we hear a loud banging on the door.

My heart falters when I see him standing there. His hair is a mess, and his eyes are filled with fear. "Don't go! God, don't do this. Don't fucking leave like this!"

"Let me go. You have to let me go!"

"I can't. I love you! I love you, and we got engaged today. Please. We'll figure this out. Just stay!"

I shake my head and turn back to the driver. "Please drive."

"Miss, are you sure?"

No, I'm not sure. I'm not sure about anything. The look in his eyes is haunting me and I'm torn between wanting to throw the door open and launch myself into his arms and running so far he can't find me.

Quinn smacks his hand against the window. "I can't lose you again. Get out of the car, sweetheart."

But then I remember all the things he said and what I know to be true. I can't go to him or cause him more pain. I have no options other than going. When I look at him, I see the past that I can't have and the future that was ripped away. It hurts too much, and I can't endure it anymore.

If I want to move forward, I have to stop looking back.

My hand lifts, touching the imprint of his pressed against the glass. "I love you too much to stay."

He jiggles the handle, and I thank God it's locked. If he touches me, if he could reach me, I wouldn't leave. He still has a chance at a wonderful life with someone else, and I have to give him that.

"No! If you love me you'll stay. Open the door, baby. Open it and let me take you back inside." He pulls at it again, but I don't do as he says. "Damn it, Ashton! We've lost so much already! Please don't let me lose you too!"

My breathing is labored as the tears stream. I've taken someone so wonderful and strong and made him beg. I hate myself.

"Drive, now," I say to the driver between sobs. I close my eyes to stop myself from seeing him like this. In all the years I've known him, he's never been like this. I did this. I'm *doing* this, but there's no other option. My hand touches the seat in front of me and through a strangled voice, I instruct him again. "Drive because I can't take this anymore. Please, go."

"Ashton!" Quinn yells, running alongside the car. "Stop!"

I can't stop or turn back, and I have to leave all of this behind me.

"I'm sorry," I say and then drop my hand.

Quinn stops running, and I can't stop myself from looking out the back window to where he stands, shoulders slumped, as I drive away.

I'm not just broken . . . I'm crushed beyond recognition.

<h1>chapter eighteen</h1>

ASHTON

"ARE YOU GOING TO TELL ME WHAT THE HELL HAPPENED?" Catherine asks as I sit at her counter, hiding from everyone in my life.

"No."

"Where's Quinn?"

I flinch and look away. "Where I left him."

When I got in about four hours ago, my eyes were so red I could barely see out of them. I'm sure I scared the shit out of her since I didn't call or tell anyone I was coming. But Catherine didn't push, she brought me inside, put cold washcloths on my face, and gave me a glass of wine—at ten in the morning.

"Did he hurt you?"

"No."

"Did you guys fight?" She pushes again.

"No."

Catherine takes the wine glass away since I'm on refill number two, stopping me from being able to stare into it. "Okay, then you're going to have to explain or give me more than one-word answers."

"He proposed, okay? Well, he sort of deemed us engaged

if you'd like to know the truth. He said these amazing and won- derful things, as though everything is going to work itself out because he declared it." This is when I can't hold back. I can't breathe. It all hurts too much. "He can't just decide, Catherine. He doesn't get it. I'm not me anymore!"

A moment later, I'm in her arms, sobbing into her chest, soaking the cotton shirt she's wearing. I'm falling apart, I did what I thought was necessary. I gave Quinn a chance at a life and a family, so I should feel better.

"He loves you, Ashy. He loves you even if you're not you," she practically croons.

I hold on to her, if I let go, I'll crumble to the ground. I'm so alone, even more so than before. Who even knew that was possible?

In my heart, I know I did the right thing. I feel it in my very core, but it was the last thing I actually wanted.

Quinn gave me something to breathe for. Without that, I don't know what I'll do.

"He can't love me. I can't take everything away from him. He'll never have kids or a wife who isn't this shell of a person. What do you think will happen in a few months when he's really done with it? I already see it wearing on him."

"You're seeing things that aren't there, Biffle."

"That's just it, all I see is the past. All I see is everything we could've been. When I see the hope in his eyes, it kills me. I love him so damn much, but I can't stop hurting when he's around."

She rubs my back. "He isn't trying to hurt you."

I lean back, raking hands through my hair. "And that's the worst part. He loves me, and it's *me* who is hurting us both. So I left. I did the only thing I could think of."

I hate myself for it. Shame washes over me, bringing me lower than I already was.

"You left?"

"Yes. I had to go." I don't tell her how or what I did. I'm too ashamed.

God, what I wouldn't give to feel numb again.

"But no one knows?"

"No, only you and Jackson . . . and Quinn."

Catherine sighs and chews on her bottom lip. I know she's thinking and trying to make sense of this. It's hard for people who haven't had the same life experiences to think they'd make the same decisions. It doesn't work that way. For the longest time, I said I would never do things until I had weighed all my options.

I know that, to her, his proposal was the promise of forever.

I don't see it that way. I think it was what he thought he needed to do.

After a moment, she touches my hand. "Okay. What do you want me to tell everyone?"

I glance at her, not sure what she means. "About?"

"Well, you can hide here, but everyone is going to be worried."

I sigh and step back. "Tell them that I need time."

"And are you going to go back?"

I know the answer is not what she wants to hear. I'm too much of a coward to go back, and if I have to look at him, I won't be strong enough to resist him.

"Can I stay for a bit?"

"Of course. Jackson and I love you and we would never tell you to go, but I'm worried."

I've been distant with her the last few months, and I can imagine she is struggling with that. We've never been that way with each other. Our friendship has always been strong and honest. When we've been at our lowest, we reach for each other. I've not done that with anyone. I've pushed—hard.

"Thank you, Cat. I'll be okay."

"You don't have to thank me. You're my best friend, and I love you. If I can help, then I want to."

Jackson comes out of Erin's room. The two of them share a look and then Jackson speaks. "Quinn has called twice. I told him that you were here and okay."

I huff. "There goes me hiding out."

"He's not going to come here," Jackson says quickly. "I told him if there was anything wrong, we'd let him know. If I didn't tell him you were safe, he'd be on a plane right now."

Because he can't take a hint. Because he thinks he can save me or whatever. "He has his out, I wish he would take it."

"It sounds like he's worried and he loves you," Cat jumps in.

Jackson nods in agreement. "He called everyone, and it's been a bit of a panic."

"Gretchen sent me a text about an hour after you arrived, and I let her know you were okay."

I groan and look up. "So, everyone knows I'm here?"

Catherine rolls her eyes. "No one knew where the hell you went, only that you took off in the middle of the night. Gretchen was a mess, so was everyone else. In case you forgot, a few months ago, we had a friend go missing."

"I didn't forget. I was there for it all."

"Yes, and so you should understand more than anyone why this would kind of raise some red flags."

I start to cry again. The emotions of the last twenty-four hours have drained me completely. "I'm sorry!"

"Ashton," Catherine's voice sounds like it's about to crack, "please don't cry."

Jackson clears his throat. "Why don't I take Erin out for a walk and some sun? Maybe you girls could use some time to watch movies and cry?"

"You just put her down." I weep.

"She's not asleep yet, it's fine." Jackson looks as though he's ready to grab the baby and run out the door.

Catherine smiles, and I turn away, feeling awful. "That sounds great, babe. Thank you."

"You have no idea how lucky you are," I tell her.

Catherine's eyes fill with sadness. "I'm well aware of the kind of man I have. It's you who doesn't know what you walked away from."

No, I know what I lost, someone equally as wonderful as Jackson.

"Do I wake her?" Catherine's voice sounds worried.

I roll over and look at the clock. It's one in the afternoon. I've been here three days and haven't really moved much. I got up this morning to eat since Catherine was hovering over my bed.

Fuck it all is my new motto.

I thought I could walk away and figure out a way to go back to nothing . . . that was a myth.

In fact, everything sucks and hurts more, so I stay in bed, crying and hating everything.

"Ashton?" She peeks her head in the door. "Are you awake?"

"No."

"Well, asleep people don't talk."

I groan and roll over.

"You need to get up. Gretchen and I think you've sulked enough."

"Good for you both."

She huffs and opens the blinds. "It'll be good for you too. You smell, you haven't eaten much, and I'm worried you're trying to somehow kill yourself."

"I'm going to kill you if you don't leave me alone."

Catherine doesn't seem to care about my threat. "Okay, you can try, but you're wasting away, so my money is on me. I could always call Quinn and let him know how you're acting."

His name doesn't bother me.

Nope. That stabbing pain is from hunger.

It has nothing to do with him or how much I miss him.

It's not like I spend most of my dreams imagining us together with that ring on my hand.

"Not like he'll care anyway." I pull the blankets over my head.

"You're right." She laughs with sarcasm. "It's not like he's called me, Gretchen, Liam, Jackson, Mark, and anyone else under the sun to get updates on you, which, you know, are that you're sleeping and moping."

I sit up with a bolt. "You told him that?"

"Why would you care?"

"I don't! I'd rather give him no excuses to care about me."

She shrugs and then sits on the bed. "Why would he? You left him because you don't love him."

"I never said I didn't love him."

"Then why did you leave in the middle of the night when he begged you to stay? Why did you get in a cab with the man chasing it down to try to make you talk?"

My eyes flash as I realize she knows what happened.

"Oh, yeah, I found out the whole story, so . . . no more hiding, Ashton."

Catherine turns on her heels and walks out of the room. I wish I had more self-control than to follow her out, but I lack that. She's itching for a fight, and I won't let her have the last word.

"I'm not hiding!"

"Bullshit. Now tell me what the hell is going on. You come here, and I have never seen you so broken, I didn't know what to do. I thought giving you some space and time would make you talk, but you haven't. You've retreated right back into that shell you were in before."

"The fuck I have! If I did, I wouldn't hurt or cry. I would be fine, but no, I'm here, in all my goddamn pain without any solace."

She rolls her eyes. "Spare me. What the hell happened that night?"

Spare her? Whatever. She wants to know? Fine. I'll tell her and then she can see that I'm not crazy, I'm finally making sense. "I left him before he could leave me. I saved him from a life-time of regret and waiting for me to ever be over everything. He doesn't really want me to wear that ring since he has no idea what I am now so how could he?"

Her eyes fill with disgust. Catherine has always been my best friend. She's called me out, held me up, and has never shied away from a fight. I should've known this wasn't the right place to go.

"Who the hell are you to decide that for him? How are you suddenly so all knowing in what's going to happen? You're a mess, and you've given up, why? It's easier than fighting? Well, fuck that shit. You're right about one thing—you're not who you were. You've been to hell, and when that happens, it has a way of changing a person. However, that doesn't mean that you get to choose what others want."

I shake my head, feeling a fury I didn't have before. "Screw you."

"No, screw you. You came here for a reason. You ran away, and I'm . . . I'm always going to be here for you, but you have to figure out why you're so scared. Is it because you're angry or is it that you're holding on to whatever excuse you can find to sabotage your life?"

"I'm everything!"

"Good!" Catherine yells back. "Be everything. Be *something*! You haven't been anything at all for a while, and I think that's why you're here instead of with the man who loves you. Do you really think he would walk away from you?"

At some point, I think anyone would grow tired of being with someone who can't even make themselves smile. I thought shutting down would make it easier on both of us. Then, I felt again.

I felt his hands, his heat, and his love, and it scared the shit out of me. I don't want to feel because then I'll be empty again. I will remember all that I lost and all that will never be.

Jackson walks in, sensing the room and clearly unsure of what to do. Eventually, he goes to stand by Catherine. She places her hand in his, and my stomach flips. I had that—or, I could've.

Suddenly, I'm angry again. I wanted that, but my life went to shit.

"No! That's the fucking problem, Cat. He'll stay out of obligation or whatever misguided feelings he has—not because he loves me. That's what would've been the saddest thing of all. He would've stayed so he's not *that* guy, right?"

"What guy?" Jackson asks.

"The guy who leaves his girlfriend after she loses their baby and becomes a crazy person. We both could've died. He was kidnapped. I almost died in surgery. We were stupid to think that we could make this work. Quinn was right in the beginning when he said love made him weak."

"Stop it," Catherine chides. "You're being overly dramatic and, I'm sorry, but I'm going to call you out. Love doesn't make you weak, and you don't believe that for a second."

I believe that I'm going to punch my best friend, that much is real. "When did you become such a bitch?"

"Day that you became a martyr."

I flip her off and then turn, my chest aching. People can judge me, I accept that, but not her. "I'm sorry, but before I loved that baby, I was fucking fine!"

Catherine moves closer. "No one thinks you're weak. We think you're grieving and giving up. Quinn was taken, and I'm sure that fucked you up. I know what it's like to think you're going to lose a man you love."

Jackson comes over and places his hand on my shoulder. "It's not easy being in a relationship with guys like us. We're impulsive, protective, stupid, and often think we're Gods when we're just as mortal as you are. Quinn took a risk, and it was at a time I think you needed him most."

"It's not about his job," I try to reassure him.

Catherine moves in. "Isn't it? You almost lost him, so you think it'll be a bit easier to give something away than have it taken again?"

That's not what this is. I'm not protecting myself because I'm worried I'll lose him that way. I'm sure that he'll leave. I know that he's going to get to the point where he can't stand to deal with my constant state of depression. Maybe one day he'll see a little girl on her daddy's shoulders and wish he could have that, but he can't.

Because I'm fucking broken.

"I don't know anymore, Catherine. That's the thing. I don't know what I'm doing, and I don't know what's right. I hurt all the time. I want it to stop."

She moves closer, cupping my cheeks. "Then you have to forgive yourself and see that you did nothing wrong."

chapter nineteen

I STARE DOWN AT THE TEXT MESSAGE, READING IT FOR THE hundredth time.

Ashton: I'm sorry. I know I don't deserve your forgiveness, but I'm sorry I did that to you.

I close my eyes, wishing the words were something other than that. As soon as I got it, I hopped on a plane. There's no clear reason why, and I have no idea what I'm going to say, but I have to see her. She broke my fucking heart. Now, I'm outside Jackson's home, prepared to get some answers about what exactly she's sorry for.

I knock on the door, my head spinning in a million different ways. There's only one person who can make sense of this, but nothing good will come of my showing up here.

A second passes before the door opens and Ashton is standing in front of me—her hair a mess and her eyes swollen. A part of me is happy to see she looks like this. If she were smiling as though this meant nothing, I might've lost it.

The shock in her eyes is clear. Catherine didn't tell her I was coming. "Quinn?" Her voice is pitched high in surprise.

"I got your text."

She rocks back and forth from one foot to the other. "Oh, yeah, I, um . . . I thought that maybe you didn't want to speak to me."

"I'm not going to yell at you, but I thought I should reply, and what we have to say to each other was worth more than a text, don't you think?"

Her lips part, and she nods. "Right. I wanted to call, but I was . . . well, I was afraid." She takes a step back and opens the door wider. "Do you want to come in and talk? Catherine and Jackson aren't home, but they have beer or we can go out and talk?"

I don't fucking know. Looking at her like this is fucking with my plan. I was going to come, say my peace, and leave her just like she did me. But she's broken enough already, I can't do it more. When she left me, I got in my car to chase her down. I got a few miles outside of town and stopped. Ashton made herself crystal clear, and there I was, doing exactly the opposite.

Nothing I was saying or doing made a difference. She sees what she wants, and I can't change that.

Still, I need to stay strong. I've done enough caving already. "I'm not planning to stay long."

After my call with Catherine last night, I realized that I can't love Ashton enough to make her better. It's not realistic or fair to either of us. She is making a choice to let our loss consume her, and I can't fight this battle for her.

Ashton clears her throat. "Then let me start. I'm sorry."

"For what?"

Tears fill those blue eyes, and I fight back the urge to comfort her.

"For all of it. I never should have left you like that."

"No, you shouldn't have. There's a lot I came here to say,

not to hurt you but because I can't move on until I say it, and I deserve that much."

"I know you do and you have every right to be angry." Her voice trembles as I watch her control slipping.

"You're damn right I do! I fucking love you, and I wanted to marry you. I have spent the last few months trying so hard to make things right for us. I've given you space, love, and understanding, but you spit in my face. I changed my entire life for you, and it wasn't enough."

Ashton shakes her head as she steps forward. "It's me who's broken. You did everything, and I . . . I've lost myself and can't handle it."

"You think you're the only one who lost the life you dreamed of? You think I didn't experience the same kind of grief? I loved our baby. I love you, and I lost you both, but one was by choice."

The baby didn't choose to leave us. It was unfair and something that I can never make right. I've struggled with that since the day it happened. The guilt of knowing I wasn't there or that maybe I could've prevented it if I had made different choices haunts me. The difference between Ash and I is that I chose not to let it consume me.

"You deserved better than what I did."

"I've been through just as much hell as you, Ashton. I was fucking kidnapped by a guy who was supposed to be my friend. I was held while I knew that something was happening to you. Can you imagine how the fuck I felt? No, you've been too consumed with your own grief to even see mine. You know what, though? I was struggling as much as you, but I put aside my own shit to be there for you. I tried so hard to give you what you needed, but it was never enough."

As angry as the words are, there's sadness under it all. I'm pissed, but more than anything, I fucking miss her. I hate knowing she's not there. Everywhere I turn, I see a piece of the life we had.

She looks down at the floor, and I feel like such a piece of shit, but she needs to hear and own this too. "I don't want to be this way. I don't want to look at you and remember how scared I was when I found out you were missing. Or relive the cab ride where I was cramping and terrified I was going to lose the baby. I'd like for all of this"—she wraps her arms around her middle—"heaviness . . . to stop weighing me down. When you put that ring on my finger, all I could think about was how much I wanted it at one time and how the happiness you had putting it there would fade away."

"I've fought as hard as I can for you, Ashton. I would've fought until I drew my last breath to show you that the life we lost didn't have to mean we lose everything. If I thought that you wanted me, I would still do it. But you made it clear that I'm not what you want. I'm the reminder of the past you can't have and the future you refuse to embrace." When I take a step toward her, my body vibrates with the need to touch her.

But I deny myself.

If I do, I'll find some fucking excuse to stay, and I can't do that. I'm all for combat, but this isn't my war—it's hers.

"You have no idea how much I wish your fight would change things," she says, and a tear slides down her perfect face.

I fight every instinct to gather her in my arms. Even now, after she fucking destroyed a part of me, I never want to see her in pain. I want to be the one who takes it from her and gives her joy. I've changed so much, just to be good enough for her, and in the end, I wasn't.

"You have no idea how much it could've, if only you wanted it to."

"One day, you'll thank me for this."

I laugh once because that's the most ridiculous fucking thing I've ever heard. "No, I don't think that's ever going to be what I do. I'll bring your things to Gretchen's so you can do whatever you want with them." She releases a strangled sob, and I speak before I lose my nerve. "I had this made for you a few weeks ago, and I had planned to give it to you when we were settled in the house." I pull the small gift-wrapped box from my pocket and hold it out to her. "I'm going to work a job with Cole that takes me out of the country for a while, and who knows when I'll see you again."

"You're leaving?"

"There's no reason for me to stay."

I can't sit around and pine over her. If she doesn't want to move forward with me, then I'll do it my way. I spoke with Mark about going back to where Aaron was taken so I could see if there was any additional information. It'll give me something to focus on and hopefully find a way to help him. There are lapses of time that Aaron can't remember, so he's filled in his version of what happened. I'd like to give him that back.

"But—" She starts and then stops. "How long will you be gone?"

"Indefinitely." The word reverberates around us, leaving an air of finality that maybe we both need.

Then I give her the box and turn around, leaving behind something far more precious than the jewelry inside. I leave her—forever.

chapter twenty

ASHTON

I STARE AT THE BOX.

It's been an hour since he left, and I've done nothing but replay his words in my head. He's leaving to go back overseas. After he gave up his entire life for me. He got out of the military, lived with me, was the man I begged him to be, and this is what I've done to him.

He'd rather go thousands of miles away than run the risk of being close to me. Not that I blame him.

God, what have I done? How can I be so stupid? He's everything I've ever wanted, and I walked away from him so I didn't have to feel. I was so naïve to believe I could control everything.

There was no way I could keep this up, and I should've told him everything. I should've run after him. I should've begged him to stay and talk more.

I've been telling myself what I was doing was the right thing, that leaving him was the only option I had to make all this hurt stop. Now I'm in worse pain than ever, and I miss him.

I miss him so damn much.

I miss the way he smiles or says my name. I miss the way his hands are soft against my face and how he wipes my tears. I want his arms around me, keeping me together when I'm falling apart.

I lost everything.

A few minutes later Catherine walks in. "Hey."

"Hey."

"What's that?"

I touch the box, still too afraid to open it. "My past and the mess of a future I've made."

"That's an awfully important box then."

Yeah, it is. "Quinn came."

"I figured he would."

I glance at my best friend. "You knew?"

Cat doesn't even appear to be apologetic. "Sometimes when one best friend sees another acting like an idiot, it's up to that friend to put a plan into motion. Just so we're clear, you're the idiot."

I roll my eyes. "I really am."

"Did you fix it?"

"No." I sigh. "I didn't. He's leaving for Afghanistan or Iraq or wherever he can go to be away from me."

Her eyes fill with sympathy. "That's what Jackson said last night. I'm sorry, Ash. You know it's not too late, unless you want it to be."

My fingers glide across the box, and I wonder if it's the engagement ring he gave me. If it is, I worry about how I'll feel about it. I hope that maybe one day, I'll see that ring again, in another way. If it's not the ring, then what? Will I lose it? Will I go backward? There's no roadmap for grief, and I don't trust myself. I decide that I don't want to open it until I'm better.

Whatever it is that he's given me, it means something, and I want the minute I look at it to be the same. I have choices, and so far, all I've done is choose wrong. Getting in that cab was the biggest mistake I made. I've lost him, and this time, it feels different.

Maybe it's because I was convinced that I was doing this for us or that I'm just this broken, but him leaving has brought a whole new set of emotions.

I pushed him away so hard that he's willing to put his life in danger to give me space. I can't let him do that, and I know, without any uncertainty, that if something happens to him, I will never forgive myself.

Quinn believed in me. He had faith when I had none, and looking at this box makes it clear that he always thought I would get better. I had to make the choice.

My gaze lifts to Catherine as my emotions bubble up. "It's too late to set things right with Quinn, but it's not too late for me to start to live again."

Catherine's smile is soft. "I'm glad you say that because you can't go on this way. You're so smart and beautiful and, as much as you're going to hate my saying this, a child isn't everything, Ashton. Life is everything. Love is everything."

"I lost him."

"Maybe so, but you can still try to make amends."

"Can I?"

"If you're really ready to face everything, I think anything is possible. Quinn doesn't hate you. He loves you so much that he's willing to let you go so that you don't have to worry about him. He's fought so hard to be a good man and deserving of you, and if you could manage to look past your own hurt and pain, you'd see that he's trying again to give you a gift."

"I don't even know where to start."

Catherine takes my hand in hers. "You start with forgiveness and deciding to let go of the past. Can you do that?"

I will always feel the loss of my child. It will live inside me, but it doesn't have to be the only thing that survives.

"I really want to."

Relief flashes across Catherine's face. I can only imagine

how worried she's been. She was right when she said that this isn't me. I'm not a wallow-in-the-shit kind of girl. I don't usually get beat down, so when I was, I had no idea how to get back up again. I still don't know that I can, but I'm going to try.

Right now, there's a sliver of hope that maybe I will be okay, and that is what I'm holding on to with both hands.

"Did you open it?" she asks as her chin juts toward the box.

"No."

"You know, whatever is in there, it won't hurt you unless you let it."

I nod. "I worry it's the ring."

"And so what if it is?"

"I worry I'll want to keep it."

She touches my hand. "I'm more worried you want to keep him."

My eyes well with tears and I bite my lower lip. "I never really wanted to lose him. I didn't know any other way. I was so scared, Cat, and when he said he was going over there, it was like something inside me snapped. What if . . . what if it happens? What if he is killed or kidnapped by someone again? What if I never see him again and this is how he'll always remember me? But, more than that, I don't want my entire life to be defined by a tragedy."

Now that I've said the words aloud, I can't sit. I get to my feet, not having a plan or idea but knowing I have to move. There's somewhere I should be, and it's not here. It's with Quinn.

"Well, I guess the only question that really matters is . . . what are you still doing standing here?"

My eyes widen, and I rush over to her and kiss her cheek. "You're the best friend anyone could ever ask for."

She grins. "I know, I'll drive you to the airport and you can tell me all about how wonderful I am."

"Deal."

I'm in the car on my way to Quinn's house. I'm not sure what to say . . . hi, sorry I've been a massive idiot. I love you. I want to get better. Please don't leave me.

None of that is fair to him. He's put up with months of my distance, only to have me rip away the only bit of hope he had. Never once in all the time we were together had he ever treated me that poorly.

I spent the time on the flight thinking about how I can change. The first thing is I need to prove that I actually want to get better. It's not going to be easy or fast, and I have to accept that losing my child and the ability to have children is going to be something I struggle with for a long time.

It was the one thing I've always wanted, and it was ripped away from me.

I've hurt so many people, I see that now. I'm not sure I can ever atone for the damage I've caused to Quinn, but I'm going to die trying. As for everyone else, I hope they'll see that nothing I did was intentional. My heart was so broken and my grief was smothering me.

The only thing I can do is move forward, and try to make amends.

One of the ways I plan to do that is to show everyone I'm ready to try. I can't live in the past and there is something I can give back to help other women not feel the agony of not being able to have what they want.

The person who can help me is also owed an apology. It wasn't Clara's fault, but I took it out on her.

I bring the phone to my ear and wait for her to pick up. "Ashton?"

"Hi, Clara."

"Hey, I'm shocked to hear from you, is everything okay?"

When we last talked, I was emphatic that there was no way in hell I was going back to the lab and was upset that she even asked me to help out in Virginia Beach.

"Everything is . . . well, it's going to be. I want to apologize to you. You've been an amazing friend, and I've been a bitch. A big one."

She chuckles. "You've had a reason to be."

"No, I haven't. Sad, sure. But not . . . this."

"I appreciate the apology, my friend, and I accept. But it's truly not necessary. I'm glad to hear your voice. Have you found a job or anything yet?"

Here's where my stomach clenches. I doubt the lab offer is still there, but maybe there's a chance. "About that . . . I wanted to ask you about the lab down here and if they still might need help. I can't commit to anything long term at this point, but I'd like to help on the case you mentioned."

Clara didn't give me much in the way of details, just that they were having a few issues we'd encountered with eggs prior to insemination. Since our lab was the one to have a breakthrough on it, they called us for help, only I wasn't there. Clara explained that I was in the area, though, and she'd reach out.

It's not my job to know about the patient's reasons, but this is their last chance.

I understand that feeling all too well now.

"Are you sure?"

"No, but I'd like to help. If I can't have children, it doesn't mean that others shouldn't."

Clara falls quiet for a few. "You know that there are other options for you too. It was way too soon to discuss them, but when you and Quinn are ready, I'm here."

"Quinn and I . . . we broke up and I fucked up so bad."

1 2 3 4 5 6 7

"I'm so sorry. Grief and loss take major tolls on couples. It's why we have Sarina in-house for counseling."

Sarina and I didn't interact much outside that one time when a patient tried to storm the lab after she found out her eggs weren't viable. That was . . . horrible. She blamed us for ripping away her chances, cried uncontrollably, and Sarina helped calm her.

Clara is always pointing out that Sarina would've helped me, but I wouldn't even let her near me.

"Do you . . . do you think Sarina knows someone here?"

I swear, I can hear Clara smiling into the phone. "I'll ask her."

"Thanks."

"Ashton," Clara says quickly. "You have no idea how much this call means to me. I've been worried about you."

I sigh. "It seems I've done a good job of making everyone worry. I'll be honest, I'm not better. But for the first time, I feel like no matter what happens, I'll find a way through it."

"That's all any of us can do."

"Thanks, Clara."

She's too good to me. Just like everyone else in my life.

"No problem. I'll send you the information for Dr. Danton so you can get in touch to see if you can help. I'll reach out to him as well . . . in case you lose his number."

"You know me too well."

"I do. Take care and don't be a stranger."

"One more thing," I say before she can hang up.

"Yes?"

I release a heavy breath as I prepare to ask the question that I didn't think I'd ever want to know. "Can you tell me . . . the baby we lost . . . I'd like to," I stammer, trying to keep myself from breaking down. "I'd like to give the baby a name."

Clara is quiet for a moment and then she clears her throat. "Would you like to know the gender?"

"Please," I say around a breath.

"It was a girl."

I close my eyes, letting the tear fall down my face. "Thank you."

"I'm sorry, Ashton. Please, don't ever be afraid to reach out to me. I'm your friend, and I care very deeply about you. Don't ever forget that."

"I won't," I promise.

We hang up right as the driver parks in front of the house. I do my best to push my tears aside and hold on to the words she said.

A girl. It was a little girl, just like I always thought.

I stare at the house, trying to place why there's a sense of ease that's washed over me. I've only spent a few minutes inside it, but it feels like home.

It's not the house, it's the person inside. Quinn is where I belong—always.

I exit and make my way to the door. I don't have a key or a plan, I have only hope and a lot of apologies.

I ring the doorbell, but no one answers. I could call him, but I don't want to give him a reason not to come home, so I sit on the steps, looking out at the ocean.

There are families out near the water, enjoying the sun. I can faintly make out Natalie's house. I remember what she said about coming by and that she thought it would be good to be close. She deserves an apology too.

I gather my purse, put my bag over on the corner of the porch where no one will touch it, and make my way down.

The sand feels good between my toes, and I recall the last time I was at the beach with Quinn. We were so happy. He was excited about the baby and I was ready to move down here for him. I remember the smiles and how he carried me off the beach as we laughed together.

There's a noise that stops me, and I glance up to find a little girl screaming as she runs. Aarabelle is outside her house as Quinn chases her. She goes in circles and then stops and then jumps with her hands out as if she's going to tickle him, and he takes off.

I stand watching them, my heart beating loudly. There's no sadness in the moment he enjoys his niece, and she's clearly happy with her uncle. They keep going and then he starts to run my way but halts as soon as our eyes meet.

Aarabelle keeps running and then stops beside him. "Auntie Ashton!"

I lift my hand to wave. "Hi."

She darts toward me, her blonde ringlets bouncing in the wind as she barrels at full speed. I squat down and wrap her in my arms.

"I missed you," she tells me as she plays with my hair.

"I missed you too."

I wonder if anyone can resist the love of this child. She gives it so freely you can't help but take it. I hold her close, and she moves her hands to my cheeks. "You look so pretty."

"Not as pretty as you."

Quinn walks our way, his eyes not moving from mine. I release a heavy breath and smile at Aara. "Do you think you could go inside and give Uncle Quinn and me a few minutes?"

She looks over to him and nods. "Don't make her cry, Uncle Quinn! Princesses need to smile and Auntie Ashton is like Ariel and she'll go back into the ocean."

I fight back a smile, and he shakes his head. "Uncle Ben is the beast, Uncle Jackson is Prince Charming, and now I'm Prince Eric?"

She shrugs. "Princes are nice. Promise you'll be nice and not make her cry?"

Quinn looks like he's on edge, but he'll never be anything but perfect to that little girl. "I promise not to make her cry. Go tell *Athiar* I said you need ice cream."

"Really?" She beams.

"Yup, two scoops. Don't let him skimp on the sprinkles either."

Aarabelle grins with mischief and takes off.

The two of us stand here as I wring my hands and I try to think of what the hell to say. No matter what the words are, it's about the intent. "Hi."

"Hi."

"I didn't know you were here when I started to walk, but I'm glad you are."

He nods. "Why is that?"

Because I'm a fool and will do anything to get you back.

"Well, you came to me to say some things, and I wanted to respond."

Quinn looks out at the ocean and then back to me. "Seems like we do better speaking when one of us flies across the country."

"Or one of us realizes how stupid they were."

chapter twenty-one

ASHTON

THE TENSION IN MY BODY IS ALMOST AS THICK AS WHAT surrounds us. We're both on unsteady ground, and as much as that scares me, I'm trying to embrace it. Hopefully, he knows that it's me who is stupid, not him.

Quinn doesn't seem to trust me, and I can't blame him. I wait for him to meet my gaze, and when he does, I can see that he's doing everything he can to keep himself calm. "Why are you really here?"

"When I lost our—daughter, it was devastating to me. I didn't know who I was anymore because my entire life has been about this one thing. It's who I am and who I thought I was meant to be. I made babies and then I couldn't—and didn't want to—make anymore for anyone else."

"You said daughter," Quinn points out.

I nod. "It was a girl."

His jaw is tight, and he stares at me. "How? How could you keep it from me?"

"No," I say quickly. "I didn't know until today. There's so much to say, but it was a girl, and I wasn't ready to know that until now. You see, I felt so lost, Quinn. It was a loss of self, and

I thought that if I could lose you, then it would be final. I would be able to create this new version of Ashton. One who didn't hurt constantly. One who wasn't always thinking about the baby that would never be. I couldn't bring myself to know if it was a girl or a boy. I needed to move on. If I could simply erase my past, then I could have a future."

"Then what the hell are you doing right now? Trying to let me know we're done? I know that. I'm moving on the way I need to now."

I shake my head and touch his arm, but he pulls back. "I'm telling you that I don't want to erase my past. I don't want to make a new anything, you're what made me whole . . . I can't breathe without you."

He lifts the corner of his lips and huffs. "Ashton, I don't know what this is, but there are only so many times I can delude myself into thinking we can work. Maybe you were right when you said we were destined to fail. I was so sure that I could change, but I'm still the same guy I always was."

"No, you're not. Look at what you've done for me."

"Done *for* you? I think you mean *to* you! I fucking failed you!"

He never failed me and I need to make that clear. "I failed you and us. I'm the one who went into my deep hole of depression and tried to take you under."

"I wasn't there. I wasn't there when you needed me."

"And I haven't been there since then. You couldn't control what Aaron did, and I couldn't stop myself. It's not your fault, Quinn. It was just the way things went for us."

Quinn moves closer. "And now?"

I shrug. "Now, I'm going to start to climb my way out of the hole. We don't have to go back in time—hell, we can't, but we can maybe find a way forward."

He lifts his hand, brushing back my hair that has blown in my face. "That's all I want for you. I heard you when you said looking at me caused you pain, and fucking hell, Ash, it's why I can't allow myself to stay."

Tears fill my gaze, and my lip trembles. All I want is for him to stay. If I ask, I know he will—and not out of obligation but out of love. There's a very deep part of me that wants to be selfish, but then that's all I've been since we lost the baby. It's been about me and my pain. I forgot that there were two people struggling to get through it all.

"I understand." I choke on the words. "When do you leave?"

"Two weeks."

His hand drops, and I shove back the tears. I have to be strong for once. I reach into my purse and pull out the box that he gave me. "I didn't open it. It felt like something I wasn't meant to do on my own." I look into his blue eyes, praying that I can get a little more time with him. "I was hoping that maybe we could talk about everything and then, maybe, we can open it together?"

He clenches his jaw, and I can see the confliction stirring deep within him. He's angry, and rightfully so, but he also still loves me. Just as I love him. I'm not sure which of my transgressions have pissed him off this time.

"What could you want to talk about? Do you want to live through all the hell we've been through again? Do you want to talk about how you lied to me?"

Lied? "What did I lie about?"

"When I asked you if you were happy about the ring, you didn't say you were freaking out and planning to run away in the middle of the night."

The regret that fills me causes my lungs to ache. I did that to him, which is unforgivable. "You're right. I did lie to you, and

I could tell you it was my grief, which it was, but that doesn't really excuse any of it."

He drops his head back, looking at the sky. I wait for him to say what's on his mind. When he looks at me again, I try to keep it together. I'm on the verge of tears and I hate that I ever hurt him. "You know what the worst part is? That right now, I want to haul you into my arms and say to just forget everything."

That has been the saddest part of this. Our love has never waned. In fact, I think I love him more than ever, but I feel undeserving of it all. I was so sure that I would lose him and that part would break me. The delusions of anger, inadequacy, and self-loathing were so real that I couldn't see myself in this relationship.

And here is where I have to earn back all the trust I've lost. "As much as I want that, and I do, I think you and I have made that mistake before."

Quinn nods. "A few times."

I take a step forward. "I need to get help before I put you through anything else."

"I've said that a few times as well."

He has. He's tried so hard to get me to open up to someone. "I didn't listen, and I'm sorry. I called Clara, and I'm going to help at the lab here in Virginia Beach. That case . . . it's weighed on me. I think it's what made me freak out, and then you proposed and, well, you know what I did. I'm so sorry, Quinn." This time, the tears do fall. There is so much regret inside me that it can't stay contained. I destroyed the best thing I ever had—him.

"You're really making it hard not to kiss you."

"I love you, and I want you to know that, when I left, I felt as though I was being pulled in half. Everything hurt, and it still does, but it wasn't because my heart wasn't yours. You have to know that."

"Fuck it," he mutters and then pulls me into his arms, not giving me a second to think. His lips press down on mine, and he holds me there.

I don't move. I wouldn't dare to. He's kissing me, and I want to freeze time. If this moment could continue forever, that would be just fine. I'm in his arms, his lips are on mine, and there're no plans of me going anywhere.

His hands glide up my back, and a low throaty growl comes from his mouth. He starts to let me go, but I don't let him. My hands grip the back of his head and keep him there. I'm not strong enough to really hold him, which means he must want this as much as I do.

Quinn seems to catch himself and leans back, breaking our connection. "I shouldn't have done that."

"Don't say that."

"I'm leaving, Ashton. I'm leaving, and you know that."

"I do, and I don't blame you."

He laughs. "I didn't realize until now that you might understand it. I can't resist you. I might try, and I might hold up for a small amount of time, but I'm unable to deny you. No matter how many times I tell myself differently, you're the one thing in my life I can't walk away from, which is why we keep going around in this circle."

He's right, and it's why I had to walk away in North Carolina. I couldn't tell him no. I loved him and knew that I'd never get better if I stayed. It makes sense that he feels the need to be away from me now.

Still, I want to spend whatever time he has left together. We've been through so much, and there's a real possibility that he might not make it home.

"Will you do one thing for me?"

He looks as though he's in pain. "Depends."

I smile. He's smart not to commit himself. "Will you please spend the next two weeks with me? I know you're going to leave, and I will do my best to accept that, but I'd like us to heal a little too. We've hurt ourselves, each other, and if you're going to go back where it's dangerous, I'd like us to be in a good place."

I wait for what feels like a lifetime.

"Where are you staying now that you're back here?"

"I hadn't gotten that far, but probably with Gretchen."

"You can stay at our place."

"But—"

"You don't have to, but they're newlyweds and I'll be leaving in two weeks. You can use the house since I paid the rent for the year."

"And where will you stay?" I ask with fear. I'm not sure if I'm afraid of him saying there or somewhere else.

If we're in close quarters, then maybe I can convince him to stay. If we aren't . . . how will I feel being in a home surrounded by his things?

He brings his hand to my cheek as though he can't stop himself. "With you."

chapter twenty-two

QUINN

HE'S HERE. SHE'S IN FRONT OF ME, AND FOR THE FIRST TIME since we lost our . . . daughter, she doesn't look as though she's hopeless. I'm not sure what to do with it, but I can't stop staring at her.

When I flew out to California, I had no idea what the point was, but if this was the end result, then it was worth it. Ashton is finally accepting that she needs to deal with it all.

"Do you want to go up to Liam's?" she asks as I drop my hand.

"Yeah, I'm sure they'll want to see you since there's no doubt Aarabelle told them. Hell, I won't be surprised if we see nose and fingerprints on the window from Natalie trying to watch."

Ashton laughs, and the sound makes me feel as though I won the lottery. It's been so fucking long. It tears me apart that it is only coming now because we're over and I'm leaving. Freeing her was the right thing to do. I could've begged or fought, but it would've kept her in that cage and she never would have found the strength to break out. Now she can spread her wings and fly.

"Well, let's make sure she doesn't have a flat nose."

We start to walk toward the house, and I fight the instinct to take her hand in mine, but then Ashton reaches out and wraps her fingers around my arm. I look down, and she notices what she did and then drops her hold. "Ash . . ."

"I'm sorry, it was . . ."

I stop walking and take her hand. "Don't mistake what I was saying. I fucking love you and would give you anything you asked for, but I don't want to hurt you."

Jesus. All of this is becoming so fucking complicated. I crave her like a drug. She's everything to me, and before she walked out that night, I would've continued to take hit after hit. I would've overdosed if it meant that was the only way I could have her. I would've endured the constant need I have when it comes to her. She's my addiction, but it wasn't me that was dying from it—it was her. And I can't fucking do that to her.

The only way she'll survive it is by making sure I don't relapse.

"I know, and I'm aware that you're leaving, so I won't get my hopes up."

I nod. "Good." Then I think about two weeks in the house with her and not touching her. I thought I lived through hell before, but this is going to be a whole new realm of it.

"Quinn?"

"Yeah?"

"Why are you being so nice?"

I look down at her, wondering how she still doesn't get it. "Because no matter what, I love you."

"I love you too." Then Ashton's eyes turn sad. "It's too bad love isn't enough for us."

It is and it could've been, but we didn't allow it to be.

"Well, this is an interesting turn of events," Liam says with a smirk.

We're on the deck, the girls are inside playing princesses or whatever game Aarabelle has demanded, and I'm enjoying a beer—or, at least, I was. Liam's face when we walked in was worth a million words. The look I shot him back caused him to keep them to himself.

Not even two hours before she appeared, we were working on his car and I was telling him all the ways I was over her.

I lied.

"I'm still leaving."

Liam snorts. "Sure you are. So, she's going to stay in the house while you pack up to leave on a mission that isn't even a mission?"

"Yup."

"And you're not at all worried that you'll both end up naked?"

"I'm not worried." It's not a concern, it's a guarantee. Not because it's a good idea but because it's Ashton and me—it always happens.

"Glad to hear it. Here I thought, oh, my idiot best friend is going to make a mistake by thinking it's not a problem that he and the woman he wanted to marry a few days ago is staying with him. But you're not worried, so why should I be? It's not as though you both don't have self-control or haven't been through hell and probably need each other more than usual?"

"Do you like to hear yourself talk?" I toss back.

"It'll be fine. I'm sure you'll stay in separate rooms, but wait, you only have one bed and a couch, which means you'll sleep there?"

"You're going to sleep in the ground if you don't shut up."

Liam laughs. The fucker forgets that I've kicked his ass in

every hand-to-hand combat training we've ever had. I'm not afraid to remind him.

"You and I have never held back with each other, and I don't know what the hell to say this time. If it were Natalie, I'd be doing the same thing you are, so I can't say shit there. However, I need to remind you that this is a really bad idea. Your head isn't straight since the whole incident, and you're a fucking liar if you tell me it is."

How the hell could it be? Aaron was my friend—or, at least, he was supposed to be. He'd held and drugged me when I needed to be with her the most. I've done what I could to forgive him, but the truth is that I never will.

"I'm not taking another rotation to see him," I say, hoping he knows what I'm talking about.

Liam nods. "I'm struggling to go there myself. Aarabelle asks about him, and I'm having a tough time not telling her that she'll never see him again if I have anything to do with it."

I've told the guys everything that I remember and how I brought up his daughter, but there was one part I've left out. I didn't think everyone deserved to know, but Liam does.

"You know part of his reasoning was that Ashton was pregnant and he was trying to help make sure history didn't repeat itself."

Liam's beer bottle lowers from his lips. "Meaning his history?"

"He said how Cole takes everything. His wife, kid, best friend and then he said how he was ensuring the same didn't happen to me. You know, Lee was pregnant when he had his shit go down, when he got back she was with you and . . ."

"And what? I was going to move in on your pregnant girlfriend?"

"I guess."

He curses and shakes his head. "It's hard to remember that he's not him anymore, you know? Aaron came back, appeared to be working through things, and then he snapped a few months back. It was as though he didn't realize any time had passed. He'd show up here, asking for his wife, and Lee didn't know what to do. He thought she was still pregnant and that Aarabelle wasn't his daughter."

I hate that he was going through that and never said a word. Not that I know what I would've done, but I would have at least listened to him. Liam is a good man, one whose values override any of his own wants. He'll do the right thing no matter how much it costs him. Having to go back in time and relive it all had to weigh heavily on him.

"Why didn't you tell me?"

Liam's eyes fill with regret. "Do you think you're the only man in the world who suffers with guilt? It's been years, and still, I look at my wife and wonder if I'm not the biggest bastard who walks this earth. Telling someone wasn't something we wanted to do, but I think him coming to the house and seeing us, having to explain what happened over and over, is what pushed him over. Aaron and I could never be the same after all that happened, and in that respect, some of the things you said to me were right."

"I don't think he snapped because of you, Liam. I wasn't right about anything I said all those years ago either. He was a fucking asshole to do what he did to Lee before he was held hostage. She's lucky that you came into her life."

"I'm sorry I didn't tell you about his issues. I really thought that, once we took him to the treatment facility, he'd get the help he needed."

He has nothing to apologize for.

"It's not like you knew of his plan."

Liam chuckles once. "I might have helped him if I did. You had it easy in BUDs and didn't get captured like the rest of us."

"I was far too superior of a SEAL even then."

"Yeah, okay. But in all seriousness, are you all right after it all? I know you're fine in some aspects, but . . ."

This is a subject we don't discuss. You don't go through the shit we have and not have residual issues, I don't give a shit what anyone says. Some guys drink. Some get angry and storm off. Some fuck around on their wives because they feel undeserving. And some just deal with it. I'd like to think Liam and I are in the last club.

Sure, I have dreams sometimes, but other than that, I process my shit and move on.

"I'm fine. Really, man. I think having Ashton to worry about helped me not think about it. I was trying so hard to fix things for her that I didn't have time to focus on myself."

"That's what I'm worried about."

"Look at you being all fatherly and shit."

Liam rolls his eyes. "I'm not about to lose another best friend because we don't deal with things."

Aaron and Liam were closer than we were for a long time. There was nothing those two wouldn't have done for each other.

"I'm not Aaron."

"No, you're not."

"Do you remember when he got stuck under the barbed wire at that training facility in North Carolina?"

Liam laughs. "The same one where you fell off the log when you were trying to show off and didn't know we had put oil on it."

Bastards. "You paid for that when I glued your boots shut at the top."

"Yeah, I couldn't get the fuckers to open and had to buy new ones."

The mood shifts as we start to tell old stories about training. After we graduated, we went separate ways. Liam went to California, and I came to Virginia. We weren't on the same team until much later. Now, I'm out and he's still active, but it still feels as though we're fighting the same battles.

"About Ashton . . ." He brings the conversation back around. "I know you're hellbent on leaving, but can you actually do it now that she's here?"

I take a long pull of my drink and think about it. My knee-jerk reaction is to tell him I could go without a doubt, but I'm not really sure. This is a fucking gift that Jackson gave me so I could get some time away, not because they actually want information. What I think they are hoping is that I'll be back in a few weeks with a clearer head.

She's here now, though. Two weeks of her and I sharing space, and her only hope is that I leave without anything being uncomfortable between us. Like that's even possible.

Just a few days ago, I put a ring on her finger. Sure, it didn't exactly go down the way I wanted it to and it crashed into a fiery pit of crap, but I wanted to marry her. I still do.

It took one smile from her to send me right back to my knees. I fucking told her to stay with me as though it were the only option. Gretchen and Ben, newlyweds or not, would've taken her with no questions, any of our friends would.

But I want her close. I need to see her, touch her, and see her smile. I want to know she's safe with me.

Then I think about the bomb she dropped on me—a girl. The baby we lost was a little girl. I think about Aarabelle and the little redhead child I'd dreamed of. "You know the baby was a girl?"

"Really?"

"Ashton apparently found out today somehow."

"You didn't think to ask?"

I can only process so much at a time. Her being in front of me was shock enough. "Not yet. I don't know that it even matters anyway. But . . . a girl. I would've had a little girl."

Liam stands, walking toward me with another beer. "She would've been spoiled with her uncles and father."

She sure would've been. This group of guys has zero restraint when it comes to the girls. Aarabelle owns this team, but Erin and Makenna, Mark's little girl who is still a baby, are well on their way to having us all wrapped around their fingers. It's always the females who bring us to our knees.

"I would've loved her."

Liam's hand rests on my shoulder. "You wouldn't have been able to resist. Which is why I'm worried about you and Ashton doing this again. Neither of you have the ability to resist each other either. If you're going to leave her, why hurt her more?"

I'm not leaving her. Not in the same sense. I'm leaving *for* her. This is what she wanted in a way, and it's the best I can do to provide it.

"I won't lie and say it'll be easy, but she's made it clear that she's here to heal, not for us to work our shit out."

"You really believe that?"

I shrug. "Why wouldn't I?"

"Because she watched you all night, and her eyes kept doing that . . . oh, Quinn, I love you, please don't leave me," Liam says in a horrible imitation of her.

"You're ridiculous."

"Am I? Want to wager on it?"

I'm not wagering on Ashton with him. "Fuck off."

"If you're so sure, put your money where your mouth is."

I hate his stupid ass. "And what do I win?"

"If you and Ashton get back together, you get the girl. If

you lose her, then you're going where you want, right? Either way, I think you win, buddy."

If I don't get the girl back, I definitely don't win, but I sure as fuck won't tell him that. I need to resign myself to the possibility of there not being a reunion between Ashton and me, only a place of understanding.

At least that's the lie I'm going to feed myself until I'm wheels up on my way to the desert.

chapter twenty-three

ASHTON

"I CAN SLEEP ON THE COUCH," I OFFER.

Quinn looks at me as though I'm nuts, which maybe I am. This entire plan is crazy, and I clearly wasn't thinking. How I'm going to spend two weeks with him and not end up with my heart decimated, I have no clue.

We finish doing our nighttime routine and walk to our prospective sides of the bed. Once we climb in, it's awkward as hell. Both of us lie here, looking up at the ceiling, hands on our chests so that we don't touch each other.

Jesus, this is going to suck.

Then Quinn chuckles. The sound is so loud in the utter silence that I turn to look at him.

"What?"

"This."

I smile. "The fact that we're both being weird?"

"Yes." He moves to his side and opens his arms. "Come here. If I only have two weeks, I plan to make them count."

A wash of sadness comes over me, but I push it away. Today is a day for hope, not regret. I nestle into his arms, loving the way I fit against him. He cocoons me, and I close my eyes, committing this moment to memory.

I'm not alone or overwhelmed with depression. I'm fighting my way through it, refusing to let it eat me alive. I'm sad because, if we hadn't lost the baby, his hand would be resting on my large bump. We could be lying here, feeling her kick, we might be engaged and planning the wedding we want.

That's not the reality, but it could be worse.

One of us could be dead.

"Quinn," I whisper.

"Yes?"

"I'm sorry."

"For what?"

I turn so I can face him and his hand rests on my hip. "I'm sorry I lost you."

"You didn't lose me."

I smile half-heartedly in appreciation of him trying to tell me otherwise. We both know it's not true. I lost him the day I got into that cab and left him. Even if he's forgiven me and is allowing me this time, he's not mine anymore.

"You don't have to lie to me."

He brings his hand up to my face, and I shiver under his touch. "I think that even if we were on opposite sides of the world, we would still belong to each other."

Do not cry. Do not cry.

A tear slips out, and he wipes it with his thumb. "Why are you crying?"

"Because I love you and this is all my fault."

"I think that's why I don't feel like we've lost each other, Ash. It's no one's fault."

"It's mine that you're leaving."

"No," he denies. "I don't think it's your fault or my fault. Who knows, I may come back in a few months and we might finally figure our shit out and not fall apart."

I'm going to fall apart when he leaves. I will always love Quinn and want him, that much will never change. Whether we're technically anything or not, he's mine and I'm his. He was right when he said we were infinite. My love for him has no end. If we can't find a way to be together, I'm not sure another man will ever fill that void.

"I have a plan."

"You do?"

Yeah, I'm going to make sure we're not on opposites sides of the world in two weeks. That's my plan.

"You'll just have to see, but . . . it's starting tomorrow."

Quinn pushes my hair back and then kisses my forehead. "Welcome back, *fragolina*."

I close my eyes and snuggle in closer. It feels good to have a bit of optimism.

"And this is our lab," Dr. Danton says as he walks me to the back.

This lab is much different from the one in New York. The biggest difference is that it's bright. It doesn't feel like a dungeon, and while his equipment isn't the stuff I'm used to, they didn't skimp either. I was at one of the top labs in the country, and this is much smaller, but it's well done. I sometimes wondered if all the technology was really better. Our rates didn't improve thanks to the upgrades, they improved as we developed better science.

"It's great." I smile, hoping he'll see I genuinely mean it.

"We could really use your help, Ashton. The case we're working on, Clara said you had a similar issue."

"Yes, that patient's egg was rejecting the sperm. It took a lot of work to figure out why."

"Would you be willing to come on board on a temporary basis and then, if you're happy and we feel it's a good fit, we could talk more permanent."

"I'm definitely fine with a temporary thing."

He beams, and I can see this was his last-ditch effort. "I can't tell you how much we appreciate it."

Dr. Danton starts to fill me in on the case he needs help with. I sit, trying not to let my emotions get out of control when he gets into the patient's history.

"She's a wonderful woman, and I want to help her."

I nod. "She's young."

"Yes, she developed ovarian cancer in her early thirties and came to me to have some eggs frozen. She had to have a full hysterectomy." My throat goes dry as I listen to him continue on, but I put myself back into science mode. "She married her husband during her cancer treatments, it was a really scary time for them both, but about six months ago, she came to me with a surrogate."

I nod. "But you're having trouble with the egg fertilizing?"

He grips the back of his neck and bites his bottom lip. "Yes. It was frustrating, and she asked to wait since we're down to one egg. She didn't want to try again before they were able to accept this was truly her last chance."

I know all too well about the feeling of desperation.

We talk more in depth about what they've tried and the issues they've had. I truly believe with the technique that I developed, this might work. Of course, I only have one egg to make an attempt on, but . . . they've yet to do it my way.

Clara was always behind me, she allowed me chances that some other doctors might not have, but I'm good at my job. I see things in a different way.

"I'd like a few weeks to really go over things, if that's okay?

You can let your patient know that it's not for lack of confidence, but more out of being extremely cautious."

He beams. "Wendy will be okay with that. She's not in any rush. She'd much prefer this work so we don't have to go with another woman's egg."

I try to imagine if Wendy was like me after her last failure. Did she feel like giving up? Did she think the cards were stacked against her? I wonder if she let her husband hold her as she cried or if she pushed him away. Or maybe Wendy was stronger than I ever could've been and got help from the beginning.

"Dr. Danton, I have a rather odd question, but do you have any kind of patient support services for your clients?"

Clara had really pushed that I see Sarina, the clinic's therapist in New York, but I wouldn't listen to her. Now, I'm starting to wonder if that wasn't to my great detriment. I don't want to go through the hassle of finding someone who understands trauma or grief, and if this center has one, then I'd probably be better off seeing her. She knows what the women go through during a miscarriage.

"We do, would you like to meet her?"

"I really would."

"Can I be frank?"

I smile softly and brace myself. "Sure."

"Clara and I have been friends for a very long time, and her husband, Mac, was actually the best man at my wedding. When she mentioned that you were here, I was curious. She wouldn't divulge anything other than you'd suffered greatly and it brought you down here."

"I had a very traumatic miscarriage where I had to have a full hysterectomy. I wasn't sure I could ever enter a lab again or do something that I know I could never have myself."

His eyes fill with sympathy. "I'm sorry to hear that, but you're here now."

"I am."

"Why don't we go meet the staff?"

"That sounds great."

Dr. Danton or as he wants me to call him, Greyson, shows me around. The more I view the clinic, the more at ease I feel. It has a homey feel instead of the posh New York vibe I'm used to. They're not trying to impress the elite rich socialites. They're helping the more every-day people in the area.

Not that one is better than the other . . . it's just different. And I need different.

We get to an office, and he knocks. A pretty woman with brunette hair and warm brown eyes smiles when she sees us. I instantly like her. I don't know why or what it is, but the second I see her, I get a sense of ease. "Dr. Danton, I didn't expect to see you." Her Spanish accent sounds on the last word.

"Carolina, this is Ashton, she's going to be helping in the lab as our new embryologist and then hopefully on a more permanent basis if we win her over."

Her smile is as bright as the sun. "Wonderful, you're doing us a great service, my caseload decreased when we stopped taking on new patients about a month ago, and while I've enjoyed the small reprieve, it'll be nice to have a full day again."

"I'm really happy to be here."

"She is Clara and Mac Madison's former embryologist. She's here for Wendy and Byron's case for the most part, but there's a chance of more if it is mutually agreed upon."

Carolina claps her hand. "That's wonderful! They are such a great couple, *and* you come from one of my favorite labs. I love Clara, she's a fantastic doctor who cares a great deal about her patients."

"Yes, she's fantastic, and I admire her very much. Carolina, I was wondering if maybe you had a few minutes to talk with me?"

"Of course. Greyson, do you mind if I steal her for a bit?"

Greyson shakes his head. "Not at all. I'll be in my office when you're done if you could stop in and sign some paperwork?"

"No problem at all."

With that, he takes his leave, and I suddenly feel very nervous. Carolina brings me inside the room, motioning for me to sit. "Tell me, what can I help you with?"

The sheer volume of help I need would probably scare her off, but I've run out of rope to hang on to. So, here I am, taking the chance on asking for help. If Carolina isn't comfortable talking to me, maybe she will know someone else who will be.

That statement alone terrifies me, but I don't want to spend the rest of my life in this much misery.

"I was trying to see what it is that instantly made me like you," I say as I fidget with my hands. "But I think it's that you remind me of someone I love very much. She's been my best friend since I was in high school, and it's probably why I'm able to sit in this room right now."

Carolina shifts forward. "Your best friend . . . is she here?"

"No, Catherine moved to California with her husband. I was there a few days ago, and she's why I'm here."

"Here in my office or here in Virginia Beach?"

"Both."

"I see." Her voice is soft with a bit of curiosity layered in it.

"Almost three months ago, I suffered a miscarriage that caused me to hemorrhage so much that I needed a hysterectomy. I was almost four months pregnant, and I . . . well, being a mother was the only thing I ever truly wanted in my life. I was actually going to have Clara do fertility treatments and then I slept with my ex, whom I love very much, and got pregnant with what I believed was a miracle." The tears start to form, and I struggle to speak. "It was . . . I was . . . the dream was . . ."

"Ripped away from you," Carolina finishes.

I nod. "I haven't been okay since then."

"I would imagine not."

"I need help. I can't live like this anymore. If you're not comfortable because I'll be working here, I understand, but I was hoping you might know someone who deals with infertility and loss that comes with it?"

Carolina gets up and sits beside me. "For a woman, dealing with a miscarriage is difficult, and if you're comfortable talking with me, then I would be more than willing to help you. The fact that you're sitting here right now says a lot about your strength, Ashton. I've seen patients wait years before reaching out for help, and by then, they've lost everything."

It didn't take me years to lose it all. I was able to do that in a short amount of time. Maybe I get a cookie for being ahead of the curve.

"I was on the accelerated plan." I try to joke.

"Why don't you tell me what you mean by that?"

I release a heavy sigh and unload. I didn't realize how much I went through in that timeframe, though. As I explained that day, I wonder how I haven't ended up committed. In all actuality, I probably should've been. Then I explain to Carolina everything else. The move, the job, the trip to North Carolina, and what led me back here.

I finish and feel winded. "I'm a mess, aren't I? I feel like I'm a mess."

"It sounds to me you're more together than you know. You've been through a very serious traumatic event, one that shifted the course of your life. I would be surprised if you didn't feel like you were a mess at all."

"I want to feel better."

She smiles and taps my hand. "Well, that's the first step."

"What's the second?"

"The work."

chapter twenty-four

ASHTON

WHEN SHE SAID WORK, SHE WASN'T KIDDING. IT'S HARD, and I feel as though a bus has hit me. In today's session, we recounted the entire day that I lost the baby. Step by step, I relived it. I went through my emotions as though we were dissecting a case. Carolina wouldn't relent on getting me to keep pushing and told me to "dig deeper" every time I started to pull back.

Now I'm sitting on the front deck of the house with wine, doing everything I can not to retreat again.

Which is truly what I want to do.

"Hey." Quinn's deep voice causes me to jump.

"Hey."

"Are you all right?"

His concern for me is unending, and letting him go is going to be the hardest thing to smile through.

"Yeah, a rough session with Carolina." I drain the wine glass for emphasis.

In the last three days, he's been great. He listened to me talk about Carolina and how much she reminds me of Cat. I can't remember hitting it off with anyone like I have with her. When we're in her office after everyone has left, she's not the sweet girl who waves and smiles, she's an exorcist who's removing the demons in my heart.

At least, that's how I see her.

Quinn hasn't pushed or asked, but she encouraged me to share with him since he probably needs to hear it after so many months of my refusing to let him in.

So, I'm doing my best to be an open book.

"You saw her again today?" Quinn asks with a bit of surprise.

I get up from the chair and walk over to where he leans on the railing. The sun is at his back, casting a warm glow around him. If I keep staring at him like that, I might go blind . . . he's perfect.

So, to cover the fact that I want to fall to my knees and beg him to stay, I stand beside him.

"I told you I'm going daily until she says we can scale back."

"I'm really glad it's working for you."

I lean my head against his shoulder, allowing him to hold me up just a bit. "I promised you that I was going to get help."

He rests his head on mine. "I know, and you're already coming back to me."

My heart begins to race because that's what I'm trying to do. I need him so much and want him even more. That's one thing that I'm learning the difference between. I can survive losing Quinn, but I don't want to. I chose him. It's not a need like breathing or eating. It's a want that is soul deep and can only be soothed by being with him.

I need to prove it.

I shake off the seriousness that this conversation is headed to. "Well, in order for me to ever return, Carolina says it's important to push hard in the beginning and that it should be intense. It's sort of her version of BUDs."

He nudges my shoulder. "You wouldn't last a day. The first time someone told you to drop, you'd flip them off."

"Well, according to all the movies and stories I've heard, they are mean."

"It sure as hell isn't summer camp."

I would rather never eat fast food again than go through months of torture. No thank you. Plus, they get really dirty. Quinn has told me so many stories about his training, and each one has made me wonder if he was a sadist.

"I got thrown out of summer camp." I shrug.

"Seriously?"

"The counselor was a bitch. She didn't like me thanks to the boy counselor, who was super-hot, and wanted to talk to me. I was fourteen, but . . . I knew how to flirt and shake what my mama gave me, and she didn't."

He bursts out laughing, his head falling back, and I swear I want to run my tongue down the column of his throat. I need to get a grip. "So, you did what?"

I look away to ensure I don't make an ass of myself. "I made out with him and made sure she walked in."

"And that got you kicked out?"

"No, I got kicked out because she told me not to go swimming, but his team was there, so I said fuck her and went anyway." Quinn looks at me with a mix of awe and a little bit of incredulity. "What? I don't like being told what to do."

He grins with mischief. "You do sometimes."

I blush and let out a soft chuckle. "Birthday and Christmas, buddy. That's when you get to order me around."

"Since we're going to miss both . . ." Quinn trails off, and I don't need to be a genius to know where he was going with that.

However, since our kiss, we haven't even gotten close to that again. Sure, he holds me each night, and last night, we watched *Lucifer* on television and snuggled, but that's it. Neither of us has made a move in that way.

But standing here in the sunset and being two glasses of wine deep makes it impossible to shove my need back into the recesses of my mind.

"Is that what you want?"

"I will always want you, Ashton."

At the same time, we move to each other as though we're two magnets being drawn together and there's no way we can stop.

My hand wraps around his neck, and he grips my hips as our lips meet in a crash of passion. I tangle my fingers in his hair as we kiss each other as though there isn't a choice.

And I don't think there is.

I hold on as he pushes his tongue inside, sliding against mine. I moan at the feel of his warmth and the taste of his mouth. Quinn's fingers dig into my sides, gripping me so tight I swear I might bruise, but I don't care.

I want him to hold me, touch me, push and pull me. I try to put all my feelings into this kiss. I pray that he'll feel the love, remorse, grief, hope, and forgiveness that are swirling inside me.

"God, Ashton." He moans and then his mouth is on mine again.

We kiss, and my head spins, thoughts of the past and any possible future colliding. I see it all, a life where we may not have a house full of children, but there's us. Two people who swam through the uncharted water to get back to each other. And then the dream I let build in my head stops.

He's leaving to go overseas for God knows how long.

I'm playing with fire, and I'm going to end up with more burns that scar me forever.

One of us has to protect us both from the hurt. He did it for me before, and now it's my turn to do it for myself.

"Quinn, stop," I say and then take a step back. "I want this. I want this so bad that there is literally nothing else that I could want more because you're perfect. You let me back in without questions. I'm staying in this house with you, lying beside you, talking to you, feeling you hold me and keep me together, but . . . you're going to leave, and I can't pretend that it won't hurt."

"I'm not trying to hurt you."

"I know you're not, but for the first time, I feel like I can breathe a bit easier, and . . . I'm afraid if I let you fill my lungs that, when I watch you walk away again, I won't be able to draw a breath after."

He runs his hand down his face and starts to move around the porch. "This shouldn't be this hard. I should be able to pack my shit and walk away, just like you did that night."

It feels as though someone has punched me in the gut. "It wasn't easy for me."

"No?"

"You have no idea the pain that walking away from you caused me."

I remember what Carolina said, stay in the hurt and work through it. Quinn and I have a boatload of hurt that needs to be addressed. If we can work through some of it, maybe he won't stay away too long. Maybe he'll come back when he sees that we're supposed to be together.

"You have no idea what it's doing to me knowing I'm going in a week and a half."

"Then stay."

I say the words and regret them the second they're out, but it's the only response I can give.

chapter twenty-five

QUINN

SHE WANTS ME TO STAY.

The confliction rolls around like a bowling ball, each pin an excuse that it takes out, leaving me with just one standing.

Can I roll a spare? Can I trust that the only reason I should get on the plane is standing in front of me, able to take me out?

I don't know, and that fact alone keeps it from toppling over.

"I can't stay."

Her smile is small and sad. "I know."

"Do you?"

Ashton nods. "I pushed you to this, and so, yeah, I know you can't. There's something you're chasing over there. Something that you seem to need."

The only thing I need is her, but I was what was breaking her. I'm going there to escape this and find a new way to live. One without this beautiful woman with her big blue eyes and smart mouth. She needs to do the same, and as long as we're around each other, this will always be what happens.

"All I need is for you to be happy."

"And what if you're the only thing that can give me that?" Ashton challenges.

"We both know I'm what takes it away."

Aston's lips part, and she huffs. "You're so wrong it's not even funny. You think that you take my happiness away? Idiot!" she yells and throws her hands up. "I'm in love with an idiot!" Then she collects herself. "I'm sorry. I promised myself I wouldn't ask you to do any of that. I'm sorry."

She rushes off the porch, and I hear the door close as I stand here.

I want to smile, laugh, pull her into my arms and spin her around. She called me an idiot. For the first time in months, I saw *my* Ashton. It's the woman who wouldn't shield her anger or watch her mouth. She was there for a moment before she reined it back in and became apologetic.

I head back into the house and find her sitting at the table, staring at her hands.

"I am an idiot." My voice is low and careful. I don't want to scare her off, but I also don't want to spend the time we have together like this.

"I know."

I grin this time. "We have a lot of shit to deal with, don't we?"

Ashton looks up at me. "Yeah, we do. I can't lie to you, Quinn. I won't tell you that I want you to go, but I understand it."

"Do you think it's because of our daughter?"

Her eyes shimmer with unshed tears. "I think it's from all of it, but mostly me. You struggle when you see me. I watch your eyes change, and there's a level of pain beneath it all."

"I hurt for you, *fragolina*. I hurt because I didn't give you what you needed and you had to leave me to find it. When I look at you, I see my failure to take care of the woman I promised to protect."

"Isn't it sad that we're both fighting the same thing? I feel like I failed you, and you think you failed me. In reality," Ashton says, and then the tear falls down her face, "neither of us had anything to do with it."

"I know that I couldn't stop us from losing her. But I could've held your hand after. I should've been by your side, but I wasn't. I've often wondered whether the time you had to put on your brave face was the reason you struggled so much after."

"No, God no, Quinn. It was never *your* fault. I blame myself, my body, Aaron, but not you. Never once did I think it was your fault that we lost her. Maybe we were just . . . never supposed to have her."

I sit beside her, both our hands folded in front of us on the table. I don't think that's true. "Do you think about her? What she might have looked like? Sounded like?"

My goal isn't to hurt her, but we have to talk about this. The loss of our daughter weighs on both of us.

Ashton's lips part and her voice is full of pain. "Every single day."

"I would give anything to change things," I confess.

Her big blue eyes look up at me, and I watch her emotions play out like a movie. "I would give anything to go back and undo the hurt I caused. So many mistakes I've made."

We both did. I tried to love her enough to get through her grief, and in the end, it hurt us both. She didn't deal with things and I kept thinking if I forced her to stay by my side, we'd find a way. Now I see I should've let her go.

"Loving what would've been our daughter was never a mistake."

"She deserves a name," Ashton says, her voice cracking. "She was ours and we . . . we loved her."

I think of the nights we laid in bed, laughing at the names we suggested just to outdo each other. I found it funny and Ashton's sense of competition kicked in. God, we had some ridiculous ones.

"None of the options we had before would be right."

She shakes her head. "No, definitely not. I've been trying to find something in my heart that feels right. Something that has hope and meaning."

"What are you thinking?"

"Iris or Rose."

I'm not sure what meaning either of them have in our world. "Why?"

"Iris means rainbow and there's the whole crossing the rainbow thing. But my favorite is Rose. First, because they're beautiful and you gave me roses—which helped lead to my pregnancy. With your poetic card that I couldn't resist forgiving you."

I forgot about that. It feels like a million years ago that I was sending her things like coffee and flowers just to get her to talk to me. Not to mention my version of Roses are Red.

I smile, unable to stop myself. "Rose."

My hand reaches for hers and she opens her palm to me as I lace our fingers.

"Our Rose."

We both sit here for a minute, letting the enormity of this moment come over us.

After another second, I lift our hands and press my lips to the back of hers. I needed to feel her skin.

Ashton sighs and then gives me a soft smile. "In the last four days, we've come a long way, Quinn Miller. Look at us talking and dealing with the hard shit."

"We sure have, Ashton Caputo, and hopefully, we're just getting started."

"I have faith."

I have you. I think the words and bite my tongue to stop myself. I might have her, but if—when I leave . . . I'll lose her.

"You're a fucking tool." Mark tosses some papers onto my desk.

"Good morning to you too, asshole."

"Did you even read these files? There's nothing in that region that is going to give you any answers, not that you're going there for that reason. Pussy."

I push the stack of useless info I wrote up to the side. "Then why do you give a shit about what's on the papers?"

Mark flops down in the chair across from my desk. "Because you're leaving and going to a hostile warzone for no reason."

"I have plenty of reasons."

My reasons are because she's getting better, but my staying is going to be what derails her. Right now, my impending departure is what is pushing her to keep at it.

Mark laughs and rolls his eyes. "Every damn reason you have is bullshit, and you know it. If you want me to sign off on this trip, give me something that actually makes sense."

He gets up and storms out of the room. Jackson already signed off when he said he understood and a man needs to make his choices when it comes to these things. I think he did it since I was kidnapped and he feels guilty. Mark doesn't share that sentiment.

Since Ashton returned, which I can thank Natalie for telling him about, Mark has been dragging his feet. He wanted some sort of report as to where I was going and what my plans were. Since I had no plan or really any idea of what I was going to do once I got there, I felt this was a good thing.

Then I started to look and realized there's not a goddamn thing I'm going to find.

Aaron was taken years ago. No one is going to remember him and the people who were involved are long gone.

Since Mark owns half the company, I need him to sign off as well as Jackson so I can actually get over there, but it doesn't look like that is going to happen.

I lean back in the chair, hands laced behind my head, and groan. What the fuck am I going to do now? I could always go to the California office if I need to get away. Jackson is probably wanting to expand, and I would rather be there than torturing myself here.

Then comes the next emotional turmoil that follows when I think about leaving Ashton.

This last week has been like old times to some extent. She's talking, even when it bothers her. We laugh, watch television, and God . . . kissing her brings it all back.

Last night, I had to take a cold shower before I climbed into bed with her. She scooted herself into my front so her hand sprawled on my chest, and I was instantly hard again. I want her so bad, but I won't take her. Not when it'll only wreck her when I go.

So, I jerk off each morning and take cold showers at night.

"Working hard or hardly working?" Her voice pulls me from my thoughts.

"Ash?"

She smiles and walks in. "I never got to see your office before, so I figured I could stop by to ask if you would maybe like to have lunch?"

I would eat you for lunch.

"Sure, let's get out of here."

If we stay in this small office, I will end up tearing her clothes off.

We walk out, and she waves to Natalie and Mark. Mark smiles at her and then glares at me. Asshole.

"Where do you want to go?" I ask as we get in my car.

"What about that new place on the beach with the deck off the bay? The one close to our house?"

Our house. She said our house. Not my house that she's living in or her house because she knows I'm going away, but ours.

Fuck. I'm so screwed.

"Sounds good." My voice sounds like I swallowed rocks.

Ashton is quiet on the drive, and it's clear she's working through some thoughts as she stares out the window. When we get to the restaurant ten minutes later, we pick a table on the deck, making me thankful for the unseasonably warm weather. This is when Virginia Beach is at its best. When the tourists have gone home and the locals get to enjoy the final days of summer.

"I wanted to ask you something," she says after our drinks are brought to us.

"I figured."

Ashton rolls her eyes. "I forget you're clairvoyant."

"Observant is more like it. You have a pattern."

"Good to know. Anyway, I was going to ask if you'd come meet Carolina with me tomorrow. We had a really . . . intense . . . session today. So much so that I had to leave early, and I'm still sort of shaken."

I reach across the table, extending my hand to her. Ashton doesn't pause before she places her palm in mine. "Are you okay?"

"We talked more about Aaron."

Well, that isn't what I expected to have upset her so much. Why does Aaron have anything to do with it? "And that's why you're shaken?"

"Not because of him, because of what he did."

She's not alone in that. Still, I want her to feel safe. "You know he's not going to hurt us again, right?"

"It's the fact that he took you and hurt you."

"You're worried about me?"

Ashton brings her other hand up and places it on top of mine. "I'm worried that this will happen again and that I will be powerless again."

"It means that much to you that I go?"

She nods. "It really would."

The last thing I want to do is to see a shrink. I don't believe in most of that shit, but I'm seeing how much it's helping her. I promised many times that I would do anything I could to bring her back, and if this is what it will take, I will be there.

"All right. I'll go."

She squeals and leaps across the table. Her hands cup my face, and she plants a sweet kiss on my lips.

"Sorry!" Ashton sits back down.

"Don't be. You're more than welcome to show me your gratitude like that anytime."

And just like that, I'm hard again. I should carry around an ice pack when I'm with her for the blue balls.

chapter twenty-six

ASHTON

"**A**RE YOU SURE ABOUT THIS?" QUINN ASKS AS WE PULL UP TO the facility.

"As sure as I'll ever be."

Not really. In fact, I'm not sure about anything, but after our therapy appointment, which was basically me crying as Quinn told her his version of the loss of our child and his abduction, she felt that it might be a good thing for us to confront Aaron.

I begged Quinn to forget she ever mentioned it. I don't see how looking into his eyes will help me. He took everything away. There will never be a time in my life where I will forgive him. Quinn telling us all of the details made it even more clear that he's a bastard.

Now I'm supposed to look at him even though I'm fucking terrified. I would've put this off forever, but since time isn't really on our side, we got in the car.

"He's not what you're expecting."

In my mind, he's gone from being a man to this monster that's ten feet tall and as big as a house. Since the attack, I can't help but think he would have to be in order to take Quinn, but I know that's not reality.

Quinn takes my hand, and we walk inside. We sign in, and the woman at the nurse's desk smiles a little too sensually at Quinn.

Seriously, I'm standing right here.

My thoughts are jumbled as we make our way through the hall. He never once lets go of my hand that won't stop shaking. My legs feel like jelly, and if it weren't for Quinn, I'd have toppled over.

"You're safe, Ashton."

I look up at him and try to smile. "I'm scared."

"I promise that he won't hurt you, and I'd be surprised if he had the strength to stand. Aaron has beaten himself up more than you ever could've. He's weak, sad, lonely, and dealing with more things in his head than you and I could ever imagine."

I want to believe him, and I don't think he's lying, but Aaron has taken on a form of something else in my mind. It's why Carolina was insistent that I come up here and lay this to rest. Healing comes in many forms and while the damage done to me has needed a tourniquet, I'm learning to slowly release the pressure so it doesn't bleed so fast.

Baby steps. That's what we're doing.

"I trust you."

Quinn brings his lips to my forehead and lingers there. "Good. Just remember I'm right here."

In our session, he told Carolina how he has already dealt with most of this. He has seen Aaron several times since his kidnapping and has found peace with what happened to him. I'm not sure if it's the whole brotherhood thing or something else. As they talked, they both agreed that it might help me to move past my fears for Quinn.

So, here I am.

Taking another baby step and hoping I don't fall.

We enter the room to find Aaron sitting in a chair, gazing out the window. He doesn't seem to notice that he's no longer alone or maybe he's asleep. Quinn takes another step inside, pulling me gently with him.

"Aaron," Quinn calls his name.

He turns, sees us both, and gets to his feet. "Why are you here? It's not your day."

My heart races, and I wonder if he's agitated and going to charge at us.

"No, it's not, but we wanted to see you."

"Liam was here yesterday. It's not your day."

My palms are sweating as we go deeper in the room, and I try to relax, Quinn will not let anything happen. He's not drugged or injured. We're safe.

"Right, but Ashton and I came to check on you."

"Ashton . . . I . . . I'm . . ." Aaron tries to speak.

It hits me so hard that my lungs ache. Aaron isn't maniacal and out to destroy me and Quinn. He's hanging on by a thread. Everything Quinn said was right. He's broken and sad. There's no fight in him. I don't think he could do anything to injure anyone.

"You're happy to see us," I finish his sentence.

"Surprised."

I can understand that. "Quinn and I thought maybe we could all talk?"

Aaron shifts his weight from side to side. "I was wrong. It wasn't supposed to be this way. I'm . . . I'm just not."

"You're not well."

His eyes meet mine, and my chest aches. "No, I'm not." His voice cracks.

For the first time since all of it happened, I can see a bit of what he's feeling. In my darkest hours, I was lost and afraid too. I could've turned to anger and held on to it, but I retreated. When the pain became too great, I did the only thing I could . . . I coped.

"Are you getting help?" I ask as I step forward.

He looks to Quinn and then nods. "I struggle a lot and there are times I don't remember, but I want to be better."

"I know it feels like there's no hope sometimes, right?"

Aaron sits back down. "I'm working on finding it."

"Me too." I move closer to Aaron, sitting in the chair beside him. My plans have gone out the window as I see him like this. He's not in any mental or physical condition to explain himself. And, honestly, it wouldn't change anything if I had the answers.

Quinn moves so that he's standing behind me and rests his hands on my shoulders. There's a protectiveness to his stance, and I garner strength from him.

"Why are you guys here?"

"I came because I was ready to tell you all the reasons I was angry and how I thought . . . well, it doesn't matter. I came to tell you that I'm not angry anymore. I'm sad for you. I think you went through something horrible and needed help but didn't get it. For a while, I believed that you wanted to hurt me, but I don't know if that's the truth. I think you wanted to hurt yourself."

Aaron's eyes stay on mine, and there's something in his gaze that I identify with, something that scares me. He acted in a way that would hurt others and I wonder if maybe he was so hurt that nothing could be done for him. But, deeper, I think he was screaming for help in the only way he knew how.

I felt that, by protecting myself, I was not hurting others around me, but that's not true either.

Grief can take hold of everything if you let it. I think the two of us have learned that.

"I wanted to get better for Aarabelle. Did you see her?" he asks with his eyes growing serious. "Did you tell her I miss her?"

Quinn squeezes my shoulders gently. "I was there the other day, after Liam came to see you."

"He brought me this." Aaron lifts a photo that she drew. On the top it reads: "Get Well Soon, Daddy."

I bring my hand up, lacing my fingers with Quinn's. I understand now why he forgives Aaron. He loves that little girl, and she doesn't deserve to lose anything else.

Every little girl needs her daddy.

"We're all hoping you get better," I say and truly mean it.

"I'm sorry, Ashton. I really am."

I nod quickly and then rise to my feet. "I know you are. I'm sorry too. It seems we're all hurting and maybe we need to forgive not only each other but also ourselves a bit too."

"Where are we going?" I ask as we're driving in the opposite direction of Virginia Beach.

Quinn smirks as he taps his thumbs on the wheel. "North."

"You realize that we live south, right?"

"You know, I heard that before."

We pass the Welcome to New Jersey sign, and I sit up in my seat. "We're going to Jersey?"

"That would be the plan."

"Oh my God! Why?"

"When's the last time you saw your mother?" Quinn asks.

It's been far too long. I smile so wide I worry I might split my face. I miss my mother terribly. We talk a few times a week, and she's figured out how much she loves texting. I swear, the woman overuses emoji's like it's her job. Every line has some sort of addition because she says it makes the text messages look pretty. I love her, but she's a mess.

She's asked me each day about therapy, and I reply—without emojis—with whatever happened. The amount of clapping hands I have gotten in the last week could create an encore. She's definitely happy.

"Far too long. When did you decide we were going to do this?" I ask.

"When I decided this was what we were going to do today. I sent her a text on her fancy new iPhone and made sure I put a ton of food emojis."

"Oh, Jesus. You're encouraging this?'

"Your dad is doing it too."

The fact that even with us in this weird not-together-but-kind-of-together relationship, he still texts my parents gives me so much happiness. He could've handled this all very differently. It's a testament to the kind of man he is.

"You realize she's trying to see if she can speak solely with them. Half the time, I feel like I'm playing some weird game where you have to deduce the statement."

Quinn nods. "Oh, I know, she's loving the eggplant one."

Which, of course, means something else. "She's Italian and loves eggplant." When Quinn bursts out laughing, I have to clarify. "Oh my God! The real one! Like the vegetable!"

"You went there . . . I just laughed."

I slap his arm. "Ass."

Quinn goes quiet, but there's a soft smile on his lips, almost as if he's trying to keep it hidden.

"Why are you smiling?"

He glances over at me and then back to the road. "Because you're laughing, smiling, talking, and calling me names. It's like day by day you're coming back to life."

I fidget in my seat a little. "I'm trying."

"I know you are."

"It's hard sometimes, but other times it isn't hard at all."

His hand moves to mine. "All I'm saying is that it makes me smile."

"You make me smile, Quinn. Being around you, having you be as wonderful as you've been . . . it makes me feel like there's a light at the end of this dark tunnel. I know I put you through hell, and if I could go back in time, I would. I feel grateful that, when you leave, at least there won't be animosity between us."

He nods as we both fall silent. I can see that he's trying to figure out what to say and do. I keep throwing these curveballs, but I'm hoping he'll take a swing at one.

Carolina has given me a safe place to explain my thoughts whether they're right or wrong. I'm able to talk about the baby without crying each time. I'm also able to work in the lab without feeling depressed. I'm still helping people find something they want.

The case that I'm dealing with now is so close to my own life that it's scary. I've been starting to really observe Wendy's last egg to make sure the method I want to use will be responsive. It's one of these cases where I feel heavily connected.

"What are you thinking about?" Quinn asks.

"The case I'm working on. She's a lot like me in terms of medical issues and . . . I can't help but think about it a lot."

"Do you regret going back to the lab?"

I shake my head. "No, it was the best thing I could've done. Not only did I meet Carolina but also I'm doing something I really love. This week, I was able to fertilize four egg sets for three couples. I had forgotten how cool it is. Not just the science, either. I'm changing lives."

Quinn's lips turn up and he takes my hand. "I'm glad you're doing this and that the case isn't bothering you."

I am too. "I think . . . instead of making me see what I couldn't have, it's sort of given me a new perspective."

"How so?"

I'm in no way ready to even think about going down this road, but just because I can't carry a child doesn't mean I can't have one. I have eggs frozen. Eggs that I stored when I wanted to know what a woman went through having them extracted. It was never for this intent, but . . . I could actually have my own baby.

Clara apparently told Greyson about this, and he subtly reminded me that not all hope is lost.

This is what I do for a living, and I didn't even consider it for myself. I'm such an idiot.

"Well, I could have a baby with a surrogate."

Quinn coughs and shakes his head. "You want a baby."

"Not now," I clarify quickly. "I'm saying that, in the future, there are options if I do. Before going back to work, I didn't even want to think about them because it was just too much."

"And now?"

I shrug and lean back in the seat. "I don't know. My future isn't quite so bleak."

"No, *fragolina*, it really isn't."

chapter twenty-seven

QUINN

"YOU HAVE TO TELL HIM ABOUT YOUR PROM DATE!" MRS. Caputo yells as she struggles to catch her breath. "That boy was so stupid."

"He wasn't stupid, he was . . . confused on what the proper attire was."

We've spent the entire night eating and laughing. I can see the tension fading from her parents as the night wears on.

"He wasn't confused, pumpkin, he was cheap and didn't want to pay for a tuxedo."

Ashton slaps her hand on her forehead with a thwack. "He tried!"

"How does one *try* to wear a tuxedo?" I ask, unable to stay out of this one.

They've been reliving her high school days. I never realized that Ashton wasn't one of the popular girls. I always assumed she was the queen. It turns out we lived through a very similar adolescence.

While my body has filled out, I have worked damn hard at it. I'm in the gym each day, take supplements, and I don't eat anything processed if I can avoid it. When I was a kid, I was the opposite. My head didn't fit my body, I was insanely skinny, and acne was not my friend. From the picture her parents are painting, she was much of the same.

She groans dramatically. "He didn't have the money to rent one, so he went to Goodwill and . . . well, he bought parts of it."

"Parts?"

Mrs. Caputo gets up while laughing. "I'll be right back."

"Ma! Don't you dare get that—"

She's back before Ashton can finish. "I had it framed because it's really something a person needs to see to understand."

I look down and there's Ashton in a stunning deep blue dress with a slit up the side. God, if I were a teenage boy, I would've given my left nut for a chance with her. She was beautiful even in high school. I don't see how the hell she says she was awkward.

Then my gaze moves to the dweeb standing next to her. Oh, I can only imagine what she did when she first saw him. "How long after your date showed up was this photo taken?"

"Oh, do you mean to ask if our sweet, timid, little Ashton had a fit?" Mrs. C asks.

"I did *not* have a fit. I merely told him that he could find a new date . . . probably one who was blind because there was no way I was going to prom with him looking like that."

"Real sweet, *fragolina*. Timmy shows up for his big date with the hottest girl in school and you roast him."

"His name was not Timmy, thank you very much. And I assure you, I was not the hot girl."

I look at the photo and disagree. "You were hot, sweetheart."

"It's the boobs. I got those senior year."

"God bless puberty."

Ashton's eyes blaze, and I swear my heart is about to pound out of my chest. The fire that I've loved for so long is burning bright, and I never want to extinguish it.

I've been close to telling her I'm not going anywhere anymore so many times over the last few hours. I didn't want to from the beginning, but I thought it was what was best for her. I didn't listen to her when she told me she needed space. I was so hellbent on fixing her, I thought she didn't know what she wanted.

I won't do that again.

I'm hearing her. She asked me to stay, told me she loves me and needs me.

I know that I need her.

So, tonight, I'll tell her, and I hope it makes her happy.

I grab my phone and send a quick text to Jackson and Mark.

Me: Trip is off. I'm not going anywhere.
Mark: Finally. Took you long enough.
Jackson: I'm glad. We needed you here.
Me: I appreciate that at least ONE of you was willing to let me do what I thought I needed to.

I make the jab at Mark.

Mark: Or that ONE of us is smarter than the rest and knew that you were being a tool.
Me: I really don't know why I'm friends with you.
Mark: Because I'm a goddamn stud.

"Everything all right?" Ashton asks, and I put my phone away. Mark doesn't need a response.

"Never better."

She smiles and then her father calls our attention back to him.

I'm going to tell her. I'm going to win her back. And then I'm going to marry her before she ever has a chance to run away from me again.

The conversation carried on until her parents excused themselves to go to bed. Now we both stand here, unsure of what to do next.

"I can sleep in the guest room if you want to take my bed," Ashton offers.

I shake my head. Neither of those options are happening. I'll be right beside her whichever bed it is. "I don't think so."

"You want the guest room?"

"No."

"Well, are you planning to sleep outside then?"

I take a step closer, not being able to stay away from her. Today, she was magnificent. She handled Aaron and her parents as though she were a new woman. She's still the same, but what we endured has changed her in some ways. Since she returned from California, I've been watching her learn to embrace it, day by day.

I've been waiting for her to go back to the way she was after the kidnapping, but she hasn't. At least, she isn't backsliding when it gets too hard.

She's stronger, more resilient, and I need her.

"I'm planning to sleep with you."

She smiles with a bit of a laugh. "My mother will kill you."

"I'm pretty sure your parents are aware we've had sex." Ashton seems to be at a loss for words as she takes a step back, but I'm not having it. "Not to mention they love me."

"They might, but I assure you that they won't allow this."

I take another step, smiling as her back brushes the wall and she's trapped. "Then we don't get caught."

"What makes you think I want to have sex with you?" she asks, her eyes blazing with desire.

"What are you thinking about?"

Her blue eyes shimmer with longing. "What are you doing, Quinn?"

I lift my hand, pushing the auburn strands of hair away from her face. "I'm wooing you."

"Wooing me?"

I'm clearly doing a pretty shitty job of it, but yes. I want to make her feel everything I am. She's everything to me, and I want this night to be a new beginning for us. We've been through so much, and we've made a mess of things. It's time to set it right.

"Yes. I have a lot of things I need to say to you."

A little part of her seems to deflate. "Before you leave?"

I shake my head. "I'm not leaving you."

"You've made it clear that you are."

"I'm not going anywhere, Ashton. I'm staying here, with you, and I'm hoping that you want me to."

Tears fill her eyes, and it breaks me. "You're staying?"

"I'm staying."

"And then what?"

I roam her face, trying to decipher what she's ready to hear. I'm going to do whatever I can for her. I'll give her the world if she'll give me her heart.

"What do you mean?"

"I don't know how to stop loving you, Quinn. I don't know how to make my heart not beat for you. You're the only man I want in my life, and I can't bear the thought of not being with you. So, I'm asking you what happens after you stay."

I want to grow old with her. I want to give her the life she wants.

"Then I plan to marry you and live the rest of my life beside you."

She's taken aback, but her hand moves to cup my cheek as tears well in her eyes. "I have loved you with everything that I am, and I hoped it would be enough to get you back."

"It was more than enough, Ashton. It was everything."

chapter twenty-eight

ASHTON

MY HEART IS RACING, AND I SWEAR I COULD TAKE FLIGHT. He's staying, and I didn't even have to beg him. Quinn is choosing me and us and there's nothing in this world I won't do to hold on to it.

"I'm sorry I can't give you the world or bring back what we had before." Quinn wipes away the tear that falls.

"I don't want that past."

"What do you want?"

"Us."

Quinn's eyes close as he leans forward, resting his forehead against mine. "I've only ever wanted you. There is nothing I wouldn't do to make you happy."

"Then just love me."

He lifts his head, his blue eyes staring into mine. "I'll love you forever."

If I'm dreaming, I never want to wake up. I'd like to stay in this place, dancing around the joy that is building in my heart. The constant throb that I usually battle is gone. All that I feel is hope and happiness.

"Kiss me," I beg.

He doesn't make me wait, and his mouth is soft and sensual as he kisses me. This isn't like the one we shared the other day— it's not demanding or forceful. Quinn kisses me as though he has all the time in the world to do so.

And then I realize he does.

We aren't on a timer that's ticking down. Our ground, which was once shaky, is getting fewer aftershocks.

He's going to stay.

My fingers lace in his hair, holding him as I taste his lips. Our tongues dance together, and I pour myself into this moment.

After a minute, I realize we're standing in my parent's kitchen, and if Daddy needs water, Quinn is going to need a hospital.

I pull away, my hand on his chest as I struggle to catch my breath. "We can't do this here."

He grins, his eyes full of mischief as he kisses my nose. Then he squats down and pulls me up into his arms. My legs wrap around his hips, and I hold on.

"What are you doing?" I hiss.

"Taking you to bed."

"I like the idea of that, but you can't."

"Oh, but I am."

I shake my head, knowing this is a bad idea and not sure I care all that much. I want him in every way. I want to give myself to him and have him bond with me.

We enter my room, and I place kisses on his neck as we move. "Quinn, my parents' bedroom is right next door."

"You'll have to be quiet."

I bite my lip as he lays me on the bed, bracing himself over me. "I struggle with that."

"I know, which is going to make this all the more fun."

I go to say something, but before I can, he's pulling my dress up and removing my lace thong. I am so freaking glad I shaved this morning. There's a charge in the room, electricity flows around us, bringing a slow burn to my nerves.

And then he spreads my legs and swipes his tongue against my core. I want to scream. It feels so good, and if he weren't holding my thighs apart, I would be squeezing them together. His hands are tight and strong, giving me nowhere to go and only the ability to feel.

"Quinn," I whisper, needing to let something out or I might explode.

"Easy, *fragolina*. I'm enjoying your sweetness."

My head moves from side to side as he continues to swirl his tongue in the most glorious patterns. He sucks my clit into his mouth and then releases right as I'm about to fall apart. I groan when my orgasm is so close.

I can taste the relief right on the edge, but he won't give it to me.

A sheen of sweat covers my skin. I'm hot and cold at the same time. My mind races because I need something, everything. Then he repeats the same motion. I climb, higher and higher, only to be let down right before the precipice.

"Please, Quinn. Please," I beg. My voice is strained as I fight to find my release without making noise.

He moans against me, sliding his tongue around again, but when he presses his finger into me and sucks again, I fall.

Endlessly down the mountain, feeling a freedom and weightlessness as I fly through the air. Quinn continues to suck and flick his tongue, pulling every possible ounce of pleasure from my body.

At some point in my haze, he climbs over me so his head is now next to mine. He wanted me to have to be quiet, well, turnabout is fair play and all. I push my hand to his chest, forcing him to lie back. I divest myself of my dress completely and then get to work on his clothes.

"You're beautiful."

I smile. "And you're in trouble."

"Me?" Quinn asks as though he wouldn't have an idea why.

"Oh, yes, darling. I'm not the only one who has trouble being quiet."

I remove his shirt, loving how toned and muscular he is. It doesn't matter that the man won't eat a cheeseburger because I'm devouring him tonight. Quinn grins at me as I pull his pants and boxers off.

His thick, hard cock stands at attention, and I want nothing more than to drive him out of his mind.

"Now," I say as I pull my hair over my shoulder to look at him. "Let's see how quiet you can be."

My tongue slides from his chest down the valley of his abdomen. I continue down to the motherland, making sure I lick all the way. When I reach the tip of his cock, he sucks in a breath.

I normally like to tease him a bit. It's fun watching his patience drain away until he's begging, but tonight, I don't want him to beg. I want to give him everything without games or reservation. If we were in our home, it would be different. Tonight, we don't have that luxury, but we have each other.

I take him deep, not wasting a second, and his hands thread into my hair. The muscles in his legs are tight, and if I could smile, I would.

"Fuck, Ash."

I slide up and down, taking him as far back into my throat as I can. Quinn's legs twitch each time, and I don't ease up. He may have wanted to draw out my orgasm, but I want it fast. My goal is to make him lose it, knowing it was me who brought him pleasure as quickly as I wanted.

There's power in this room, and I'm chasing after it.

"Sweetheart," he rasps between his teeth. "I can't last."

Good.

His fingers tighten, and he guides my head in a new rhythm. I move faster, breathing out of my nose as I use my tongue to apply pressure as I bob my head.

Then, when I take my hand and massage his balls, Quinn loses it.

He grabs the pillow, covering his face with it as I drink him in. He spills into my mouth and I don't stop until he falls slack.

I wait for him to look at me, there's sweat on his face and he's struggling to breathe. "That was . . ."

"Quiet."

He smirks. "Just think, once I get you home, I'm going to make you scream."

"I look forward to it."

"To what?"

"Us going home."

Quinn must like that answer because he rolls back on top of me. Both of us are still naked and it's very clear what he plans to do.

I love that he always wants me. Neither of us seem to ever be able to resist the other. His eyes stay on mine and then he lowers his mouth to mine.

"I love you," I say before he can connect our lips.

"Not nearly as much as I love you."

I don't think that's true, but arguing with him is not what I'd like to do right now. Our lips meet in the sweetest of touches before he places kisses on both of my cheeks, my nose, my forehead, and then over each eyelid. I run my fingers across his coarse stubble and then down to his chin, savoring each moment of this.

There are no thoughts of running away. Nothing haunting me other than the need to feel him inside me.

"Make love to me," I say to him softly.

Quinn lines himself up and pushes gently. His eyes close as if he can't help it and his lips part as a deep sigh comes out. I can feel his sense of contentment flowing through him. And I too have found my way back home.

Because with Quinn is the only place I belong.

"So, new job, back with Quinn, failure to call your best friend when you returned," Gretchen raises a brow and waits.

"You'll need to find a way to get over it."

She grins. "I already have since you lost your mind and all, but it sucks that my husband was the one to tell me you were back."

"I didn't lose my mind."

Gretchen leans back in her chair. "What do you call it, Ash? You were a zombie and Catherine and I were planning an intervention."

I hate that my friends were worried, and if it were one of them, I probably would've already had the intervention or kicked their asses back to normal. In some ways, I've learned that while I love the whole tough-girl, say-what's-on-your-mind thing, I don't really walk the walk of it.

"I call it a refusal of reality."

She smiles and laughs. "Did Carolina tell you that?"

"No, I made it up, thanks."

We both laugh and catch up on her life. She and Ben are doing great, which I expected, and she's thinking of getting her license to practice law down here, which I didn't expect. She seems to love working for Jackson and Mark. I really thought she'd stay there.

"Do you think you'll leave Cole?"

"No, I love it there, but Ben and I work together all day and then come home and there's no real separation. I'd like to start a family . . ."

She trails off, and I reach for her hand. "You don't have to feel bad about starting a family, Gretchen."

"I don't want to hurt your feelings."

I have the greatest friends in the world. I've always known I was lucky, but I didn't know how much.

"You're not," I say with so much sincerity that it almost brings tears to my eyes. She's not hurting my feelings for wanting to start her family, and that thought alone is beautiful.

"You look wonderful, just . . . happy and, oh, Ash. I was so worried, and I want you to be okay."

I feel wonderful. Quinn and I got home yesterday, and he spent the entire day making good on his promises to make me scream. After a lot of really fantastic sex, we started making the house into a home.

It wasn't until we were in the middle of it that I really saw how much I needed it. We were living out of boxes in New York for a while and then I felt so lost that I didn't care about this house. Looking at it through a new lens, I really can appreciate everything that Natalie made sure it had.

As we unpacked, I felt as though the clouds were lifting and the sun found its way through our windows.

"I'm not all the way there, I won't even pretend I am, but I am happy. Quinn and I are back together and things are good. I'm working again, and I can talk about babies without my heart feeling like it's being ripped out. There are moments when it's hard, mostly on days that I know would have been a mile marker for her or if I think about what she might have looked like."

"She? I didn't know you knew."

"It was a girl. Clara told me the other day when I was finally able to ask."

Gretchen's lips lift into a small smile. "Well, if she was anything like her mother, she was sure to be a hellion."

"I wish I would've had the chance to know," I say with a hint of wistfulness.

"I do too."

I nod, knowing she hates this for me just as much. "Let's talk about anything else."

"Shoes?"

My best friends know me so damn well. "Shoes are always a good topic."

chapter twenty-nine

ASHTON

~Two months later~

"**A**SHTON," GREYSON CALLS AS I'M WALKING TOWARD THE lab.

"Hi there."

"How are you?"

I smile at my new official boss. "I'm great, you?"

"The same. Busy as ever."

"Did your daughter pick her wedding dress yet?"

Greyson rolls his eyes and shifts a little straighter. He absolutely hates her fiancé, so anytime we mention the wedding, he bristles.

Which only makes every member of the staff ask him more.

I am now the official embryologist for this lab. Yesterday, I signed my contract and Clara wept on the video screen since it terminated any possible employment with her. I'll miss her so much, but I love my job. I love this lab and the people I work with. It's filled with friendship and caring. Everyone knows each other, and we even have lunch every Friday together as a team. There is never any bickering, not that there was in New York, but this is like a family.

I didn't know the nurses in New York. I didn't know anyone other than a few doctors and my lab technicians. It was meant to feel separate and at the time, I liked it. It worked fine for me, but here . . . that is not even a possibility.

"Oh, Greyson, don't make that face, it'll get stuck like that."

He glares at me, but there's a smile with it so I know I have nothing to worry about. Although, I don't even think Greyson knows how to get angry. Still, it's always the quiet ones.

"I came to talk to you about something serious."

I cease my teasing immediately. "Is everything okay?"

"Yes, actually, I spoke with Wendy and her husband and they're ready to go forward."

"Really?"

I wasn't sure that this case was ever going to come to fruition. Then I started to wonder if this wasn't some ruse that Clara concocted in order to get me to take this job. She knew I wouldn't be able to resist the call to science.

Doing something once can be a fluke, but being successful a second time would solidify the methods I used.

If I fail, though, that would be devastating.

So much rides on this one egg.

"They apparently did some research on the embryologist who is helping out and, well, found out she was kind of a big deal."

I roll my eyes. "I'm a hot mess."

"Regardless, you have the only case where you were able to have a successful pregnancy."

I blush under his flattery. "Do they have questions?"

"Probably a million."

"I would expect that. Most of it is a lot of steps and procedures that no one outside a lab would understand."

Greyson nods. "I'm sure, but they're coming in today, and I would like you to meet with her."

"Of course."

Anything to ease her worries.

"Great, they'll be here in twenty."

"Twenty minutes?" I basically screech. "You didn't think I should get a little bit more of a heads-up?"

"Do you need to prepare?" he asks.

"Well, no, I guess not. But still."

I don't really see patients since describing scientific procedures isn't exactly a titillating conversation that anyone cares about. Not that they are coming for that.

My breath comes out in a deep sigh. Time to pull it together.

"You'll do fine. They're good people."

I nod since I don't trust my voice.

Greyson walks off, and I head to the lab where it's quiet.

Wendy and Byron are a sweet couple from what I'm told. One that has entrusted me to give them the one thing they want most. She's been through hell and back, lost everything, and now wants a slice of heaven.

She also scares the shit out of me.

What if this doesn't work?

What if I fail, will it set me back?

I've been so happy, and Quinn and I have settled into our new life with ease. There have been tense times, but thanks to Carolina, we're finding that we can communicate so much better.

She's taught me a lot about myself and what I need to do to get through it.

I grab my phone and send him a text.

Me: I'm worried. I'm apparently meeting the couple for the case I came here for.

Quinn: You're going to do fine.

Me: I wish I had your confidence.

Quinn: You do, you have to believe it. However, I'm happy to leave work for a noon-er and give you any "confidence" I got.

I burst out laughing.

Me: The lab is a sterile environment.

Quinn: You have patient rooms.

You know, it would be kind of fun. I shake my head, wondering what the hell is wrong with me? I just got this job officially and I'm thinking of screwing my boyfriend for confidence.

Me: I'll take your "confidence" later tonight.

Quinn: Now I'm hard.

Me: You're always hard.

Quinn: That's because I'm always thinking of you.

Me: I love you.

Quinn: I look forward to you showing me exactly how much later.

I roll my eyes and put my phone away right in time for Carolina to knock on my door.

"And what are you smiling at?"

"Quinn."

She grins. "I'm heading down to meet Wendy and Byron, want to walk with me?"

I nod. "Sure."

While I would love to believe this is just her being sweet and not wanting to walk alone, I've learned that everything she does is a teaching moment. I only see her once a week now, and our session feels more like two friends talking than anything else. We laugh a lot, and she even brought a bottle of wine the last time.

I'm not sure I'm still allowed to be a patient—or that I ever really was—but I love her dearly.

She's nothing like my other friends. It's a much more mature relationship, and over the last two weeks, our conversations have become much less one-sided.

"How is Quinn?"

"He's doing well. He's working on a new set of training guidelines, which I care nothing about but listen to him drone on for hours and hours."

Carolina giggles. "Much like I'm sure he thinks about your laboratory work."

I scoff. "I'm very engaging."

"Sure you are."

"Why did I agree to walk with you again?" I ask.

"No clue, but here you are."

We get to the conference room, which is set up almost like a living room. Carolina and Greyson designed it to feel welcoming and less like an office. This is where most of the bad news is delivered, so I doubt the patients care, but I can appreciate that our staff does.

A girl, who is about my age with long blonde hair, jumps to her feet. She moves quickly toward me. I take in how beautiful she is. I can tell she works out because there are only four people in the world who get to look as perfect as she does without working for it—Gretchen being one. She moves with grace and the poise of a dancer. Her face is delicate and she has these thick dark lashes that are so freaking stunning I'm instantly jealous.

When she stops right in front of me, her excitement is palpable. "Are you Dr. Caputo?"

I smile and shake my head. "I'm Ashton, but I'm not a doctor."

"Oh, I'm sorry." She turns and looks to her husband, waving her hand at him to come closer. "This is my husband, Byron. We're . . . well, we know all about your work, and Dr. Danton speaks so highly of you. We almost went to the clinic in New York when we heard they were the best with this, and then . . ." Tears fill her eyes, and she struggles to catch her breath. "Then you came here."

"Please don't cry," I say the words with a smile. "You'll ruin your mascara, and we all know a woman covets her lashes."

Wendy giggles and drops her voice to a whisper. "They're extensions because I cry . . . a lot."

"I do too."

Byron reaches his hand out. "It's nice to meet you."

"You as well, please call me Ashton. I'm just a biologist, and while my family wished I got my doctorate, I'm not as stuffy as these two." I wink and toss my thumb toward Carolina and Greyson.

We all sit around the couches and start to discuss everything. I'm as thorough as possible without being boring. Mostly, my goal is to make them feel comfortable. They can hold off longer if they'd like or forge ahead. I'd like them to feel that my confidence is as strong as ever, even if it's not.

There are many variables that can affect the success rate, and I want them to understand that, while I've done this before, it doesn't mean we'll have the same outcome.

"So, there is a fifty-fifty chance either way?" Wendy asks while gripping her husband's hand.

"Yes. There are no guarantees, but Dr. Danton and I are very good at what we do and will do everything in our power to give you the best chance."

"But you didn't do this with him before?" Byron asks and then turns to Greyson. "No offense, Dr. D."

"None taken," he assures them. "Ashton worked in the lab with another endocrinologist, but we are very close colleagues, and Dr. Madison has shared all of her notes and research. I do want you both to know that if I weren't confident in my or Ashton's abilities to handle this, I would refer you to another clinic who could."

Wendy sighs. "You think this is our best chance?"

My voice is strong as I answer her question. "I think it's not only the best time but also that you're in the most caring location. I loved where I was before, so please don't take this as a slight, but it's clinical in New York. Here you have the support of the entire staff. I truly believe that no matter how far science has come, there's something to be said about the human heart. Our team here treats each patient uniquely, and if we didn't think we would be successful, then we would be laying things out very differently. It's a chance, but it's truly your best one."

"I wish you understood. I've lost so much."

I'm not one to overshare, especially with a patient, but I get her. On a base level, I can feel her pain and fear. She and I are kindred spirits in many ways, and who knows, maybe one day, I'll be in this same predicament. I would want to know the people walking this road with me really got what it meant.

To me, Wendy isn't a case file.

She's not a statistic or an award to try to obtain.

She's a person with a dream of being a mother. Her heart is laid out right before us, and it's our job to let her know that we will take care of it.

I look at Carolina with a small smile and she nods imperceptibly.

"Wendy," I say with a shaky voice. "I suffered an unimaginable loss about five months ago. I had a miscarriage with complications, which left me unable to ever have a child. It nearly destroyed me.

I'm telling you this because I do understand. More than anyone. You see, all I've ever wanted was to be a mother, and there's nothing I wouldn't do if it meant I could have that back. There is no one in this industry who will work as hard to be successful as I will."

Tears fill her eyes as she gets to her feet. "Thank you."

Carolina takes my hand in hers on the table and squeezes, her voice is barely audible. "I'm proud of you."

When Carolina rises and walks to Wendy and Byron, I feel raw and exposed, but in a good way. My chest may be tight, but I'm so glad I said it.

Then a hand touches my shoulder. I look up, expecting to see Carolina, but it's Wendy. "Thank you for telling me that."

"I didn't do it to gain your trust, I wanted you to know that I truly do understand."

"You know, for a long time, I didn't think we could ever have children. I had accepted it, or at least told myself that I did, and then I saw the look in Byron's eyes one day as we passed a park. He didn't say anything, but there was this . . . hope . . . and I thought I might break apart. I became obsessed with having a baby again, and now I worry . . ."

I try not to picture Quinn. I shove all the emotions that threaten to bubble up aside, this isn't about me. Wendy is a patient and I want her to trust me and my team to give her the child she wants.

"You have hope here too, Wendy."

She nods with a soft smile. "It's hard to love a man so much that you want to share a child but know you'll never be the woman to give it to him. I'm terrified that I still won't be able to even though it's not my body this time, it's my egg."

I stand, feeling as though the floor beneath me is shaky. "It's incredibly difficult. No matter what you decide, know that we'll be doing everything we can to give you that hope back."

Wendy's eyes brim with unshed tears. "You know, sometimes I wonder if I did something wrong, but then I remember that I'm not alone and none of us did anything wrong. You reminded me of that just now."

I breathe through my nose to keep from bursting out in a sob.

"No, we're not alone."

She looks over to her husband and sighs. "And you know what? He couldn't care less if we ever have a child, it's me who wants to give it to him because I love him and saw his eyes in the park that day. Byron will love me no matter what the outcome is, but I truly hope we can. He will be a wonderful father."

I think of Quinn and how he feels the same. He couldn't care less if it's just the two of us for the rest of our lives.

I'm the one who wants the full family.

"I'm the same."

Wendy smiles as though she already knew that. "That's the funny thing about loving someone. We often make ourselves crazy thinking we know what they really want, when all they want is for us to be happy."

"Well, to be fair, we usually are right."

We both chuckle. "I knew I was when I married Byron."

And I hope one day I'll be able to say the same thing about Quinn. Yes, I had the ring and then I gave it back, but maybe it's time to let him know I've changed my mind.

chapter thirty

QUINN

"You're taking her to dinner?" Liam asks as we're finishing up a workout.

"It's a date, not just dinner."

He puts his hands up with a chuckle. "Sorry, Ladykiller, I forgot you have mad skills to seduce."

I hate him.

"Whatever, Prettyboy. I'm going to dinner with the plans to propose, but if her day went half as bad as I think it did, I'll hold off on that."

"You don't trust her?"

I sigh and chug my protein shake. "It's not trust, it's timing. She met with the girl who also is her age and lost her womanly parts."

"It's called a uterus."

"Who cares what it's called?"

Liam shrugs. "Women?"

"Okay, Dr. Uterus . . . my point is that she was nervous going into the meeting, and I'd like to avoid another fuck up of a proposal. However, if we do go down that road, you need to be ready for the wedding next week."

Liam bursts out laughing. "Next week?"

"Yup."

"So she doesn't run?"

"So I can finally make her my wife. It's been a long time coming. We started dating when you and Lee did. She looks at you guys married with a baby . . ."

"Well, I'm not a dumb ass."

"Yeah, we'll go with that."

"Says the idiot who isn't married with the baby." Liam's face falls when he realizes what he said. "That was out of line. I'm sorry."

Every now and then I think about how she'd still be pregnant. I touched her belly last night as she slept and thought about how I might not be able to get my arm all the way around her by this point. And then I had to put that shit out of my mind and thank God I could put my arm around her at all.

"You didn't mean it that way, it's fine."

"Still."

I need to change the topic. "Anyway, dinner, and if she's not weird, then I'll propose and let her know we're getting married next week."

"Yeah, Ashton is totally the do-as-you-say type of girl. I'm sure she'll love having her wedding steamrolled by you."

I'm hoping she sees the wisdom in my thinking, but knowing her, she won't. Shit. He might be right on the whole shotgun wedding.

Her mother might also kill me if I don't allow her the wedding she's dreamed of. Maybe I can convince her to elope and just pretend for her family's sake?

I'll work those details out later. For now, I have to get the ring on her finger and actually have her verbally agree this time.

I won't make *that* mistake again.

"I have a feeling she won't care so much."

"Why, because you're such a catch she's worried you'll get away?"

With friends like Liam, who needs people who will insult you for real? "And you're a winner?"

He smiles as a girl walks by waving. "See, she thinks I'm hot."

"She was looking at me."

Liam claps his hand on my shoulder. "I don't think so, but nice try. Back to the issue at hand, are you sure that you'll be okay if she says not yet?"

I've tried to ask myself the same question. I mean, let's face it, no guy wants to be told no. We don't ask a girl to marry us to end up without the ring on her finger. I sure as fuck don't want to go through it again, but I love her. I want her to know that, even with the shit we've been through, I see her on the other side.

Ashton has come full circle. She's back to being funny, smart-mouthed, and voracious in the sack, which I am not complaining one bit about.

She's nothing like she was before, and that makes me think that she'll want to be engaged this time.

"She's come a long way, and while I'm not ever sure what the hell goes on in her brain, I'm pretty sure I'm reading the signs right."

Liam slowly nods. "Then I'm happy for you. You are a lucky man, and she . . . well, I worry about her."

"Dick."

He gets into his car, and I flip him off as he drives away. It's a short ride home, but I start to finalize a plan on how to make this night perfect and have the perfect end.

Ashton is home when I get there, which is weird since she

doesn't usually leave the lab until well after six and it's only four. I rush inside, worried that she didn't text me after her meeting with the couple and I have no idea how she did.

"Ash?"

"I'm in here!" she calls from the bedroom.

"Hey," I say when I see her standing in front of the mirror in a tight black dress.

Jesus Christ, she's magnificent. Her long red hair is flowing down her back and there's a glow around her. I swear that I've never seen her look more beautiful. I walk into the room, and she smiles.

"I came home early."

"I see that."

"I wanted to try on my new date dress."

I raise a brow. "Why is that?"

"Because it's pretty."

I shake my head as I come up behind her, looking at her reflection from over her shoulder. "No, the dress is nothing compared to the girl wearing it."

She leans back, not caring that I'm still sweaty and probably stink from working out. "Do you like it?"

"I'd like it better on the floor."

She turns in my arms, her hands coming up to my chest. "You need a shower."

"Are you offering to help clean me?"

"As tempting as that offer is, my sexy beast of a boyfriend, I'll skip this one and take a raincheck."

Damn. The thought of her wet and washing my back has me rock hard. I don't think I'll ever get my fill of her. "Suit yourself."

"I have big plans for us."

So do I, my love. So do I.

"Yeah? What kind of plans?"

Ashton leans in and gives me a quick kiss. "Go get yourself clean and you'll find out."

I give her a salute with a wink. "Yes, ma'am."

"At ease, sailor."

I roll my eyes, grip her ass, and pull her against my chest. I run my nose down her neck, and she shivers. "God, I fucking want you."

"Quinn . . ." Her voice is husky, and I know she wants me too.

My hand moves up her back, and I grab the zipper, slowly sliding it down so that the noise echoes in the room.

I love that she doesn't try to stop me. Her fingers glide across my skin and then her lips touch mine. I kiss her softly, teasing her and enjoying the soft sounds that escape. Ashton isn't going to take it lying down, though, she never does. My girl likes to give as much as she takes. Her tongue brushes against mine before she retreats, causing me to growl and surge forward.

There is nothing sexier than a woman who isn't afraid to use her power. Her fingers grip the back of my neck, hauling herself closer to me. I push the fabric of her dress down, leaving her standing in heels and her underwear.

I take a step back to look at her. I drink her in, each drop giving me the will to live. She has no idea how much I need her to breathe.

My mouth opens to ask her right now. I want to bare my soul to her, but she deserves better.

Her head tilts to the side. "What's wrong?"

"You take my breath away."

Ashton takes a step closer, and her hands touch my skin, branding me even more than I already am. Her deep blue eyes bore into mine, and I swear I can see myself reflected inside her. She's feeling just as much in this moment.

"Marry me," she says, causing me to freeze.

"What?"

I'm pretty sure she stole my line.

"I want to marry you."

At least that clears up any questions I had about whether tonight was the right night.

"Did Liam call you?"

"Liam?"

I shake my head. "I was . . . I was planning to ask you tonight. It's why we were going to dinner and then I had a few surprises planned."

Her lips turn up into the most stunning smile. "You were?"

I laugh and pull her into my arms. "I was. See, I have this problem that I was hoping you could help me with."

"What might that be?"

"I'm hopelessly in love with you and can't seem to imagine a life without you in it."

"Hmm, that does seem like a problem," Ashton says while running her fingers along the back of my neck. "I might have a solution."

"Does it involve you agreeing to be my wife?"

"That could be a start."

I release her and walk over to the drawer that has the same diamond ring I gave her once.

"Ashton Caputo, I planned to do this a lot more dignified than you in your underwear and me in gym clothes, but then that wouldn't really be us, would it? We're sort of messy, a lot of fire, and the most unconventional couple. With you by my side, I find it impossible to care about any of it because you make it perfect." I take her hand, rubbing my thumb along the top, and drop to one knee. "I never really asked you the last time I proposed. I was afraid of what the answer would be, but I'm not scared now. So, my *fragolina*, will you marry me?"

She bends down, taking my face in her hands as her tears fall. "Yes, yes, yes, my amazingly wonderful man who I will never let go of again."

"Promise?" I ask as I wipe the tears that rest on her cheek.

"I love you so much."

I pull her down to the floor as she giggles, but I catch her as she falls, the way I always will. "I love you more than anything in the world."

"Yeah? Prove it."

And then I do. My lips are on hers, placing a searing kiss on her mouth. After a minute, I pull back. "How much do you love me?"

Her eyes fill with so much love that if I weren't already on my knees, I would be now.

"Infinitely."

"Good, because that's how much time I plan to spend loving you."

epilogue

ASHTON

~Four Years Later~

"Y OU OWE ME! YOU OWE ME SO FUCKING MUCH!" GRETCHEN screams as another contraction hits.

"You really shouldn't curse so much when you're delivering my kid," I chide.

Her glare silences me, but I'm unaffected. She's been a little ragey throughout the entire pregnancy. Apparently, even in utero, our child is difficult. Not that I'm surprised, it's half me and half Quinn.

"I'd be careful, Ash, she might bite you." Catherine rubs her arm where Gretchen's teeth got her.

"You were trying to eat in front of me. I've been in labor for sixteen hours, I want to eat!"

It's been a very long sixteen hours too. She has to be the most hostile woman in labor I've ever met. Catherine claims she was nothing like this and it's clearly the dramatics in Gretchen coming out in full force.

"See, here's why you making lists isn't always a good thing," I explain as I cross my legs in the chair next to her.

"You are such an asshole."

"Again with the language. My kid is going to come out saying f-bombs."

"If your kid ever decides to come out."

I shrug. "She's comfy."

Catherine laughs. "You know it could be a boy."

"You know that most people find out," Gretchen chides as her head falls back. "The suspense is killing me."

Considering there was not one surprise that Quinn and I could have with this, I refused to find out. We implanted four embryos—two girls and two boys—and one took. I have no idea which it was, but I'm convinced it's a girl, just like the daughter we lost.

Quinn is convinced that . . . it's a baby. He claims that he doesn't care if our baby is a boy or a girl, but he's been insane since we found out that Gretchen was, in fact, pregnant.

I'm pretty sure Ben wants to kill him, but he also gets it. Trying to find a surrogate was hell. Absolutely hell. There is so much risk involved for the parents and the mere idea of the surrogate wanting to keep the baby sent me into crazy town.

Quinn was adamant that we find a friend or family member. Gretchen or Catherine were the only two I would consider. Since Catherine lives across the country, it really was up to Gretchen.

No one could've ever expected her reaction. She didn't even need a moment. She agreed immediately and was so happy to be pregnant without having to deal with infancy. Now, I'm pretty sure she regrets all of it.

Carrying my child apparently isn't anything like her last.

Catherine pops a chip into her mouth, which earns a glare. "You've had two kids already, what do you care?"

I stand and wipe Gretchen's forehead with the cool cloth. "Let her rest, Cat. She's beat."

"Yeah, let me rest," she says and sticks her tongue out.

There's a knock at the door, and Gretchen mumbles.

"How's she doing?" Quinn asks.

And then she growls.

"That good, got it."

Catherine walks over. "Oh, she bit me. She's a peach."

Poor Quinn, he's so nervous and Gretchen has said he's not allowed in until it's actually the birthing time. He's also only allowed to stay by her head. I laughed . . . a lot. I love my best friend, and we both can never repay her for doing this for us. If the biggest demand she makes is for him to stay outside and then by her head, we'll take it.

I, however, was not so lucky. No, I'm to be here the entire time, and she's used every minute to remind me how much she hates me.

At least now I know what some guys go through.

"She shouldn't be too much longer," I tell him. "Dr. Danton said she was finally progressing, so we'll keep you posted. How's Ben?"

Quinn looks heavenward. "Ben and I are having a contest for the most worrisome."

"Is he winning?" Gretchen asks.

"Don't think so."

"Damn, tell him to step up his game. I'm his wife, for god sake, and I'm doing all the fucking work!"

Gretchen asked that Ben not be in here, he's seen his wife deliver two children, and she worried he wouldn't be able to handle knowing that this baby wouldn't be his. So, Catherine is here for Gretchen.

I smile when Quinn's eyes bulge. "See, she's a peach—with a potty mouth."

"She is carrying our baby," he excuses her.

"Yes, this is true." I idly slide my pendant on my chain, and when he looks down at me, his eyes soften and it feels like we say so much in these seconds.

I opened the black box the day we found out that Gretchen was pregnant. I didn't want to open it sooner, for no real reason, but Quinn also seemed content not to touch it until we decided whether we were going to do this or not. Months of waiting and wondering if we should attempt it. Then we agonized over the possibilities and finally decided to try.

The first two attempts failed, and I made a promise that if it didn't work on the third attempt, I would stop trying and be happy. I meant it, at least in theory.

When Gretchen took her pregnancy test and it turned out to be positive, we went into our bedroom, pulled the box out of the safe, and, as promised, opened it together. Inside, was a beautiful necklace with two angel wings with a red ruby in the center. Rose is symbolized by the stone and the wings, he said, mirrored each of us.

I put it on that day and have never taken it off again. Rose is with us right now, I can feel it.

"You okay?" he whispers.

I nod. "I'm ready."

"Me too, *fragolina*."

I smile and lace my fingers through his.

Another contraction hits, and Gretchen groans. "Ohhh, this baby hates me. I have to push!"

"No!" Catherine and I both yell at the same time.

Even though my job is to make babies, I don't ever deliver them, and I'd prefer this to not be my first. If she has to push that means she's much farther along than we thought.

I turn my head to Quinn as I rush toward Gretchen. "Get the doctor!"

He bolts out of the room, and Catherine and I take Gretchen's hands. "You can't push yet, there's no one there to catch it," I tell her. "The doctor is coming."

She looks at me with exasperation. "Then get there with a basket because it's coming! I can't stop it. I need to push!"

"Me?"

"Well, it's your kid!"

Fuck. Shit. Okay. I have some—albeit it's from watching *Grey's Anatomy*—medical training. I should be able to do this, right? I mean, catch the baby or pretend to while I wait for Greyson and the damn team of nurses to get here.

I get to where her legs are spread and seriously don't want to look. "Ashton!" Catherine yells. "You should probably keep your damn eyes open!"

Gretchen stares at me. "Oh my God! My two best friends are delivering a baby, and it's not even my baby! This is some seriously fucked-up shit. I mean, this kid is screwed if this is the first moments he gets to have."

"She," I correct.

"Relax, Gretch," Catherine says while turning her head to stop from laughing. "We all need to be calm."

"Says the girl who is up by her head."

Quinn rushes back in with Greyson and two nurses. Oh, thank God. However, Quinn gets an eyeful because he makes a noise and then covers his eyes.

"Burned into your retina, huh?" Catherine laughs.

"Yup."

"She needs to push," I explain, not caring about those two jackasses.

Greyson smiles and walks over with all the confidence in the world. "All right, let's see if baby Miller is ready to come into the world."

I take two steps back, not sure of where to go. Do I stay down here? Do I go back up by Gretchen's head?

Then Quinn takes his place on her left and the door opens again, bringing in another hospital bed.

The nurse takes in my expression and smiles softly. "When the baby is born, Gretchen wanted you to feel those first moments, so we're bringing in a bed to be beside hers. You'll hold your baby the same way any new mother would."

I look at my best friend as tears fill both our eyes. "Get changed into a gown, Momma."

This is too much. I can't breathe, but almost without thinking, I do as she says. I remove my shirt and bra, and slip on the gown, opening in the back. She's making a lot of noise, so I hurry a little more to get back out there.

"Gretchen, when the next contraction hits, I want you to push," Greyson tells her as I round the second bed and grab for her outstretched hand.

"You can do this, Gretch."

She's tired and sweaty, and yet, when she looks at me, there's a determination in her eyes. "I love you, Ash."

"I love you too."

She will never understand the gift she's giving me. I can't ever thank her enough, love her more, or be able to repay her.

It's . . . the most selfless thing anyone has ever done.

Quinn stands behind me, one hand on my shoulder and the other on Gretchen's. "Thank you."

She smiles, and then another contraction comes, wiping it from her face.

Gretchen struggles through the next two, each of them draining her strength a bit more, but then she gives a strong push, and I hear the cry.

The perfect, most heart-wrenching cry.

Loud, strong, angry, and my entire world stops because that's *my* baby.

A baby that is a miracle.

A child I thought would never be is alive.

My tears are falling, and I haven't even seen or heard anything that's happening. All that I can focus on is the sound of our child.

"Ashton," Greyson calls my name. "Get in the bed, and we'll bring the baby to you."

I nod and then look at Gretchen. "Go meet your baby, Ash."

"You . . ."

"I'm fine." She smiles. "I'm tired, but I'm fine."

Catherine is on the other side of her, tears streaming down her face. "You're more than fine, my amazing friend."

Quinn and I climb onto the bed and his arm wraps around my shoulder. Then the baby is brought over. The nurse smiles. "Please meet your son."

"A boy?" I choke on the words.

"I always knew my boys were strong."

Before I can respond, the nurse pulls my gown down and places him on my bare chest, his tiny warm body rests on mine, and I can't stop the steady stream of tears. "Hi, sweetheart. I'm your mom and this is your dad."

Quinn touches his face, caressing our son's cheek with reverence. "He's perfect."

"He is."

I hold him close, whispering things I don't even think make sense as I drop soft kisses on his forehead.

"How is he?" Gretchen asks from the other bed. I look to Quinn, and he nods.

I get up, carrying over a child we both love. He might be my egg and Quinn's sperm, but without Gretchen, he wouldn't be here.

"Do you want to hold him?"

Her lip quivers, and I know this has to be incredibly difficult for her. She carried a child for nine months, only to hand him over, and my heart hurts a little. Whether she knew all along, she loved him. She felt him kick, heard his heartbeats, and dealt with the not so pleasant parts. She's also hormonal and exhausted. I wish I could make this easier for her. I wish she didn't have to suffer to bring me joy.

"I would very much if that's okay."

I place him in her arms and a sense of relief flashes over her. "Hi, little one. I'm your Aunt Gretchen and I'm very happy to meet you. I hope you give your parents so much trouble. Like, draw on their walls, pee in their faces when they change your diaper, puke down their back too, okay?"

I laugh and touch his face. "I will never be able to thank you enough for this."

"Oh, Ashton, there's nothing I wouldn't do for you. Just promise me that you'll never ask me to do this again."

I lean in and kiss her cheek. "I promise."

Gretchen kisses the top of his head, and a tear rolls down her face and she hands him back to me. "Here, I think someone wants his daddy."

Quinn is beside me, his eyes transfixed on our son.

I lift him and place him in his arms. Quinn's eyes mist as he holds his son for the first time. "Is that still the name you want?" he asks.

"Please," Catherine complains. "The suspense is killing us all. We had to wait to find out the sex, don't make us do it with the name."

I look down at him and smile. "Gabriel Burke Miller."

Gretchen gasps. "Burke?"

We wanted to honor Gretchen in some way. After a lot of

talk, Quinn and I found a way to do so regardless of whether the baby was a girl or a boy. "If he was a girl, we would've gone with your first name, but I thought your maiden name would be the perfect middle one for a boy."

"I . . . I can't even think," she says while a tear falls down her cheek.

"He's perfect," Catherine says. "This entire thing is perfect, and I can't tell you how much I love the two of you." Her eyes are misty as she looks at Gretchen and then me. "What you guys have done . . ."

"Don't start, Cat," Gretchen warns. "If you start crying we'll never get you to stop."

I look at my two best friends with so much gratitude in my heart that it's hard to breathe. They have been there for Quinn and I in a way that I can never express my gratitude for.

My fingers brush the delicate sprinkle of red hair on Gabriel's head. My son, my beautiful son who is here and in my husband's arms. I want to clutch him to me and never let him go. I love him so much more than I thought was ever possible.

"We'd like to take him to the nursery and give Gretchen some time to rest," Greyson explains as he approaches.

Quinn looks at me with utter horror in his eyes.

"What?"

"I can't walk with him, can I?"

"Walk with him?"

He nods and the fear in those blue eyes causes my stomach to clench. "He's too little to be moved around like this. What if I drop him? What if I trip? What if someone bumps into him?"

I smile reassuringly, a little giddy at how my big, tough husband is brought to his knees by our baby. "You won't drop him or trip. You'd never let anything happen to him, would you?"

"Never."

"No, because you're his father and you protect the things you love."

"I love you, Ashton."

"I love you more."

He looks down at Gabriel before lowering his lips to his forehead. "I love you, son."

The nurse smiles, and extends her hand to escort us over to the other room that we paid for so that Gretchen can get some rest and have privacy. As happy as I am, I can't help but feel as though I'm abandoning her.

I look back and there's a sense of understanding that passes between us. "Go be with your son," she says softly. "And get my husband for me."

"I will. Thank you."

We exit the room, and my fingers wrap around Quinn's big arm as he cradles our tiny baby. Before we enter our private room, I turn to go to the waiting area so I can get Ben, but he's already on his way in as I walk out into the hall before I can take a step.

"Is this him?"

"This is Gabriel," Quinn's pride shines through his voice.

He leans in and gently touches the top of his head. "You have no idea how many people love you, Gabriel."

"Are they all in the waiting room?" Quinn asks.

"Every single one of them."

"Well, it's time for our son to meet his insane family," I say as we walk over to the glass that looks out at the observing area.

Quinn touches my elbow, and I turn and look at him, feeling this sense of completeness I had only hoped existed. There, stands the man that I love more than anything, holding the child we didn't think would be.

There is nothing in the world that is more beautiful than this.

"Do you feel like you finally got everything you wanted."

I shake my head. "I got that when I got you, this is more. So much more."

His lips touch mine in the sweetest of kisses, and right here, holding our baby and knowing I have the most wonderful husband, a peace I'd only dreamed of settles around me and I know, that everything is exactly how it was meant to be.

bonus scene

QUINN

"UGH, I'M SO TIRED!" I YELL AT ASHTON AS SHE GLARES AT me.

"You're tired?"

Then I realize my mistake. Yes, I'm tired. Very tired. However, my wife is exhausted. She's been up with Gabriel for the last three nights while he's been sick. I've gone to work, napped at my desk, which I will never admit to, while she has been home with him all day.

In fact, I'm pretty sure Ashton hasn't slept since he came home a year ago.

"Not as tired as you, but . . ."

"But?"

"But nothing. There was no but there. It was a mistaken but." I try to back pedal before she launches something at my head.

She's done that twice already. Both times were deserved, but the last one she almost got me. I had said we should cancel the party for today, and that is when the water bottle almost nicked my head. She's planned our son's first birthday relentlessly and has spent more money than I care to know to make sure he had the party of the year. Not that he'll remember a damn thing of it, but it makes her happy, so I've learned to just go with it.

"I'm glad to hear it. Now, go watch your son and make sure nothing wakes him up so I can shower for the first time in four days before all our friends start arriving."

"You know you look beautiful even without the shower," I compliment, really meaning it.

Ashton's lips turn into a smile. "You're a charmer, Quinn Miller."

"And you're perfect, Ashton Miller."

She touches her hand to my cheek. "You're not going to play golf tomorrow."

Damn it.

Her father must've already asked her mother, who let Ashton know of our plan. Pops is all about golfing when he's down here. Since Gabriel is spoiled rotten with attention by his nana, there's no reason the boys can't go and have fun.

"You know your father will guilt your mother . . ."

She shrugs. "My father is free to go golfing, but you're going to have to take Gabriel with you because I plan on not leaving my bed. I'm exhausted, I look like shit, and I need a break."

Hmm, take the baby with me? I could do that. He's one, what possible trouble could the kid cause?

A plan starts to form, and Ash laughs through her nose as if she knows exactly what I'm thinking. "You're an idiot."

"You know, I consider that a term of endearment."

"It's not."

"Semantics."

Ashton rolls her eyes and then heads into the bedroom to shower. Gabriel is asleep on the floor, I swear the kid is narcoleptic, except at night. No, that's when he wakes up thinking the world is his to explore. We've tried everything. He's completely determined to ensure no one in this house ever sleeps.

I look down at him, so sweet and quiet, and wonder how I ever thought I knew love until him. Ashton and I couldn't be any luckier. He's a good kid—minus the sleeping. He's happy, smiles all the time, is starting to walk, and I swear he's saying *Dada*. I don't care what the hell Ashton says.

He's also the spitting image of my wife. If I didn't know for a fact he was mine, I'd think she did it all on her own. He has blue eyes, deep auburn hair, and her nose. I swear I'm in there somewhere—just haven't found it yet.

My hand pushes his hair back as I smile at him. I stand here for I don't know how long, just marveling at the miracle of my son as he's quiet.

"He's really sweet when he's sleeping," Ashton says softly from behind me.

I turn and when I do, my heart stops. She's breathtaking. Sometimes I forget just how perfect the woman I love is. We go about our days, working, trying to function in the chaos, and then moments like this take me to my knees. Ashton stands there, towel just over the swell of her breasts and one on her head. She's flush from the shower, but it only adds to her beauty.

"God, you're gorgeous."

Her lips turn up into a smile. "You need your eyes checked."

I start to move toward her. "You have no idea how much I love you, do you?"

She stands there, a seductive smile tugging on her lips. "Maybe you need to remind me."

Oh, I'll remind her, all right. "How would you like me to do that, wife?"

I don't give her a chance to answer before I fuse my lips to hers. Her body melts into mine, as passion flows between us.

Our tongues meet, both giving and taking as my arms hold her close. I love the way she feels against me. No amount of time will diminish what we share.

I love her.

I need her, and I'll never let her go.

God, this woman infuriates me most days with her smart mouth and unwillingness to make anything easy, but I wouldn't have it any other way.

She's strong, resilient, and determined, which is exactly what makes me love her.

Ashton moans into my mouth and I rip the towel away. I push her back into the bedroom, unable to stop myself. My hands cup her breasts, and her fingers grip my ass, pulling me closer to her. It's been over a week since I've had her. Seven days of keeping my hands to myself and being jealous of a toddler as he nestled against her boobs while he slept.

That is my spot and Gabriel is definitely not between us right now.

"I want you."

"I want you too," she admits.

I bend down, lifting her up so her legs wrap around my waist and start to move her toward the bed, but before I can plop her down, I hear banging on the door. And then the sound of Gabriel yelling fills the house.

Great.

"That would be my parents," Ashton says as she closes her eyes.

A bunch of cockblockers. All of them.

I look down at her, lips swollen, eyes filled with lust. "Tonight, there will be no interruptions. I'm going to fuck you—hard."

She grins up at me and wiggles her brows. "Well, now I'm just excited."

"You should be."

I release Ashton's legs and wait for her legs to steady. She bends to grab the towel and I slap her bare ass. She looks up at me with a sultry look. "I'll take some of that tonight too."

Killing me. She's killing me.

I head to the door, opening it so her parents can come in, and then move to get Gabriel. He's already crawling his way toward me as I get close. "Hey, pal, you have a good nap?"

He rubs his little eyes and nestles his head against my shoulder.

"Gabriel!" Mama C exclaims as she enters with her hands out. "Come to Nana."

He goes without hesitation. Even though Ashton's family technically lives in New Jersey, you wouldn't know it considering how much time they spend down here. I give it another two months before they announce they're moving in next door.

I shake my father-in-law's hand, and he grins. "Golf?"

"She'll kill me."

He snorts. "Son, stick with me and you'll learn that managing the Caputo women is all about finesse."

"I heard that, Daddy!" Ashton exits the bedroom wearing a blue dress and she has twisted her hair into some weird knot on her head. "If Mom hears you, you'll need to manage her kicks and punches."

He smiles at his daughter. "Hi, my sweet girl."

"Yeah, don't sweet girl me."

But there she goes, folding into his embrace, and he winks over the top of her head. The man is a freaking genius, and I will now call him Yoda.

"Well, well, the gangs all here." I smile as we get to the tent set up on the beach in front of Liam's house. Ashton, Natalie, and Gretchen went all out. There is food lining the one side, a cake that we're going to be eating for a year on the other, and a full bar—for a one year old.

My wife is a force of nature.

"Look who decided to show up to his own kid's party," Mark quips.

"I'm surprised you're able to be out here without your cane, grandpa."

Anger flashes in his eyes, but he covers it up quickly. "I'll take your confession tomorrow, my child."

Here we go. Someone needs to find out how to nullify online ordainments.

"Jackson," I say as I shake his hand. "Glad you could make it."

"Like Catherine would have it any other way?"

True. "Glad we're all being dicked around by our wives."

All of us chuckle, knowing it's true.

"Not me," Mark cuts in. "My wife knows who is boss."

I scoff. "Charlie owns your nuts, buddy."

"Maybe so, but I'm in charge."

Liam raises a brow. "Really? Want me to call her over for confirmation?"

"I'm not scared of her. Go ahead . . ."

Ben shakes his head. "This is going to be so bad."

Mark is a stupid man. Charlie will eat him alive, but it'll be fun to watch. At least we don't have to worry about entertainment at this rate.

"Hey, Char—" Liam is cut off when Mark punches him in the arm.

"Are you trying to get me killed? That woman will shoot me."

So much for his whole being-in-charge thing. In the last year, my friendship with these men has only become stronger. We're a family more than a company. Ben, Mark, Liam, Jackson, and I understand each other in a way that makes things run smoothly. There are days where we want to strangle each other, but for the most part, it's all brotherly love.

The only dark spot in our unit is Aaron. He's struggled with his choices and felt that it was best to go his own way. It breaks my heart for Aarabelle, who doesn't seem to understand her father's disappearance, but Liam and Natalie do their best to explain it. Jackson heard from him a few months ago. He said he was doing okay and was happy that he moved on and started over.

Still, no matter what hell he caused in our lives, I hate seeing a brother struggle.

Liam slaps my arm. "What about you, Quinn? Is your wife the owner of your balls?"

"What do you think?"

We look around the party and start to laugh. No guy would do this crap. If it were me throwing the party, I'd give Gabriel a cardboard box—since that seems to be the only "toy" the kid shows interest in anyway—and call it day.

"Speaking of . . ." Jackson says beneath his breath.

"What are you jackasses doing?" my gorgeous wife asks as she eyes us.

"Nothing, *fragolina*. We're just admiring the party."

"And the women who threw it," Liam adds on.

"Right." She crosses her arms over her chest.

"We were actually talking about how lucky we are to have women like you all," Ben says.

Ashton eyes all of us. "Well, all of you need to wrangle your children up so we can eat."

"Anything you say, sweetheart." I step forward, pulling her against my side and press a kiss to her temple.

"Awww, look how cute you are." Mark clasps his hands in front of him and bats his eyes. "You're like a sweet little couple who love each other so much."

Ashton flips him off as she walks away, yelling, "Suck it, Twilight," over her shoulder.

"And there's the reason I love your wife, Quinn. She's full of piss and vinegar."

"Don't I know it." I laugh.

All of us head down toward the water where the kids are playing. Aarabelle is "watching" them since she's ten and feels she is old enough to babysit. Of course, it's just the illusion she has since my mother-in-law, Liam's father, and Jackson's mom are all there as well. None of us would let her and those kids down at the water without supervision.

We're not that dumb . . . most of the time.

Jackson yells for his girls, and they don't even hesitate to come running out of the water. I swear, his kids are the most behaved out of all of them.

Liam does a loud whistle that has his kids come running. His kids think he hung the moon, so they always try to impress him.

Ben's kids just follow them, but then there are Mark's two. His daughter rushes toward him, her arms wide as he scoops her up. There's nothing that can corral his son, though. I watch Cullen as he does a fakes right and then left. Right before Mark catches him, the kid is taking off up the beach laughing.

He puts Makenna down and yells back at us. "A little help?"

Liam yells back. "We're good, you got this!"

All of us chuckle, but Ben goes forward to help Makenna up to where we all stand.

My mother-in-law brings Gabriel up to me. "Here, take him so I can help Ashton."

"Thanks, Mom."

I hold him close as we all watch Mark. I knew we'd have dinner and a show.

"Ten bucks says Cullen heads into the water," Liam bets.

"Twenty that Mark has to go in after him," I raise it.

Jackson laughs. "Fifty says Charlie has to go in after both of them."

Ben takes that bet and raises him one. "A hundred bucks says Cullen outruns him the entire time."

Sure enough, Cullen beelines to the water.

"Fuck!" Mark yells. "Really, Cullen?"

And then Mark is in the water.

My joy is cut short when Charlie appears at my side. I'm going to buy the woman a bell and make her wear it—wait. No, that's a terrible idea. "Are you all just standing around watching this?"

"It's my son's party, I'm not going in the water." Hell no. My wife will kill me if I get wet before we take photos. I'm not even allowed to sweat too much because it isn't summer and I can control it, but still, Ashton demanded it.

Charlie groans. "I swear, the men in that bloodline are all hard-headed and pains in my ass."

The rest of the women descend to where we stand. Ashton wraps her arms around me from behind. Her chin rests on my shoulder and she giggles. "Seriously, our friends are insane."

"That they are. Still, they keep it interesting, and I wouldn't want it any other way."

"Me either. I'm glad this is our life." I turn my head just slightly, and she kisses my cheek. "Really glad."

"Me too."

"Good," Ashton says with a sigh. "Since we're stuck with each other for eternity, we might as well be happy about it. This is living our best life."

I nod and look around at the people gathered around us. I have my wife, my son, a family, and friends who I would give my life for. "Yeah, *fragolina*, this definitely is, and I'm glad I'm living it with you."

Damn glad because without her, it wouldn't be a life worth living.

books by
CORINNE MICHAELS

The Salvation Series
Beloved

Beholden

Consolation

Conviction

Defenseless

Evermore: A Salvation Series Novella

Indefinite

Infinite

Return to Me Series
Say You'll Stay

Say You Want Me

Say I'm Yours

Say You Won't Let Go: A Return to Me/Masters and Mercenaries Novella

Second Time Around Series
We Own Tonight

One Last Time

Not Until You

If I Only Knew

Co-Written Novels with Melanie Harlow
Hold You Close

Imperfect Match

acknowledgments

To my husband and children. You sacrifice so much for me to continue to live out my dream. Days and nights of me being absent even when I'm here. I'm working on it. I promise. I love you more than my own life.

My readers. There's no way I can thank you enough. It still blows me away that you read my words. You guys have become a part of my heart and soul.

Bloggers: I don't think you guys understand what you do for the book world. It's not a job you get paid for. It's something you love and you do because of that. Thank you from the bottom of my heart.

My beta reader Melissa Saneholtz: Dear God, I don't know how you still talk to me after all the hell I put you through. Your input and ability to understand my mind when even I don't blows me away. If it weren't for our phone calls, I can't imagine where this book would've been. Thank you for helping me untangle the web of my brain.

My assistant, Christy Peckham: How many times can one person be fired and keep coming back? I think we're running out of times. No, but for real, I couldn't imagine my life without you. You're a pain in my ass but it's because of you that I haven't fallen apart.

Sarah Hansen for once again making these covers perfect.

Melanie Harlow, thank you for being the good witch in our duo or Ethel to my Lucy. Your friendship means the world to me and I love writing with you. I feel so blessed to have you in my life.

Bait, Stabby, and Corinne Michaels Books – I love you more than you'll ever know.

My agent, Kimberly Brower, I am so happy to have you on my team. Thank you for your guidance and support.

Melissa Erickson, you're amazing. I love your face. Thank you for always talking me off the ledge that is mighty high.

To my narrators, Andi Arndt and Jason Clarke who bring these characters to life in a way that only you two can. Seriously, that last chapter in Indefinite . . . I'm still not over it. Andi, your friendship over these last few years has only grown and I love your heart so much. Thank you for always having my back.

Vi, Claire, Mandi, Amy, Kristy, Penelope, Kyla, Rachel, Tijan, Alessandra, Meghan, Laurelin, Kristen, Devney, Jessica, Carrie Ann, Kennedy, Lauren, Susan, Sarina, Beth, Julia, and Natasha—Thank you for keeping me striving to be better and loving me unconditionally. There are no better sister authors than you all.